Beyond

A LOVE STORY

Beyond
A LOVE STORY

CHITKALA MULYE

www.whitefalconpublishing.com

Beyond a love story
Chitkala Mulye

www.whitefalconpublishing.com

First Edition, 2021

Cover design by White Falcon Publishing, 2021
Cover image source pixabay.com/pexels.com

Requests for permission should be addressed to
chitkaladitosh@gmail.com

ISBN - 978-1-63640-304-5

This book is
dedicated to my father
Late Dr. Ashutosh Mulye

Acknowledgement

I was riding a moped bike on a hot sunny afternoon. I was feeling dizzy. I was heading towards an event called 'Human Library' and had lost my way. I was terribly thirsty and was on the verge of fainting. After great struggle, I reached the venue. That was the time I met Sagar Barve, a 'human book' in Human Library. He was there to share his own experiences as gay when he had come out of the closet.

Later, as a life coach and writer, I interviewed him. The glimpses of a gay's life I got from him helped me discover an incredible germ for this novel. Sagar helped me explore the character of Sameer from the eyes of a gay person, and that's how I could step into his shoes and truly connect with gay's mind. I extend my thanks and gratitude to Sagar for supporting me at every stage during the making of this novel and answering my endless questions.

When I think retrospectively, I realize that all that effort I had taken was planned by destiny to introduce me to Sagar, who opened the doors for me to a gay person's life. I was pregnant with my first baby, and the conception of my second baby, my book, 'Beyond a love story' was on its way.

I started working on this story with my 3-month-old baby nursing on my lap and my second baby, my book, which was equally demanding, was taking shape. My third baby, my life coaching venture, was also evolving, showing me more life and relationships, helping me build my characters on the emotional canvas and painting the relationship dynamics giving more life to the story.

During that time, I was at my home in Ratnagiri, enjoying my maternity care. The story of my book started taking shape over a cup of tea with endless brainstorming discussions with my mom. My proud mom, who always dreamt of seeing me as an author, added colours to my book with her unconditional emotional and intellectual involvement. So finally, by the end of the first lockdown during the COVID-19 pandemic, my first draft was ready.

This book also got enriched with feedback from some wonderful minds. Most importantly, my mom Aditi Mulye, fully envigored with her skeptical mind, brought the best out of me. Once my manuscript was scanned through the eyes of this best story critique, my friend and husband, Saurabh Vartak, gave it a sincere read. He is a classical musician who always stays away from books but he added an emotional retouch to my novel with his review.

I would like to thank my grandparents, who passionately participated in the making of my book and enjoyed the book at every stage with their wholehearted interest.

Madhura Mutalikdesai, my best friend, has always motivated and supported me during my every endeavor. She enriched my book with her valuable suggestions and feedback.

It was only after the initial reads and scrutiny that I disclosed this best-kept secret to Rakesh Anand Bakshi Sir, who was a friend of my father. He has always guided, inspired and motivated me during my journey as a writer. Like always, he gave me his expert suggestions and helped me give some final touches to my manuscript.

The backbone of this book, Sagar Barwe shared his opinions and helped me refine some critical portions of the book to keep the detailing closest to reality.

It was then my friend and ex-colleague, Gayatri Mishra, gave me her editorial review and gave me enough confidence to approach publishers. Also, Sandeep Kolhatkar, her better half, helped me network for my post-publishing plans. Thanks to Bindu Madhav Khire Sir for his support pertaining to the social cause. Many authors encouraged and motivated me during the phase of exploring publishing options and extended moral support. My uncle Yogesh Joshi, Prof. Girish Shirodkar and Rajiv Bakshi were among them. Special thanks to my friend Kushal Luniya who supported me during my publishing stages with his inputs related to designing.

Once the book was ready to get published, many well-wishers took a deep interest in reviewing my book and sharing valuable inputs. Sincere thanks to Sahil Potdar for investing his time and effort to share a critique of my novel and providing useful insights throughout all the stages of publishing. Special thanks to paternal support, Sanjay Prayag, who shared his reviews in the end-moment, giving me a boost of confidence to move ahead. Also, thanks to Prashant Valkar, Abhijeet Kolhatkar, Sayantani Ghosh and Deepti

Ghui for sharing their feedback on my book. Thanks to Prachi Marathe, Sayantani Ghosh and Gulraj Bedi for their feedback on cover design and moral support. Thanks to Swati Phadke for her last moment help in proof reading. Special thanks to my buddies for their feedbacks on cover design and moral support, Madhura Mutalikdesai, Amit Nevrekar, Prashant Valkar, Sneha Usgaokar and Abhidnya Patharkar, for being there whenever I needed them. I also thank team 'White Falcon' for a hassle-free publishing experience.

A huge 'thank you hug' to my mom, Aditi Mulye, for dreaming with me till this dream became a reality. Her contribution to my book on intellectual as well as emotional level from the conception of the book to its publishing has been invaluable! Something even more special to share with you all. I wish to dedicate this book to my father, Late Dr. Ashutosh Mulye. I missed him at every step while writing this book, not just as a father but as a sexologist and doctor with whom I always had open discussions on all taboo topics since my childhood. Thanks to Saurabh for motivating me to keep up my spirit during all ups and downs from the day I decided to write my first book. Oh yes! How can I forget my sweet little toddler Ahana. Without her cooperation, this book wouldn't have materialized. A huge thank you kiss for the angel of my life!

Preface

A man and a woman come together to procreate and live as family to bring up their children. The marriage system rests on this foundation with the ethical boundaries set by the human being. These vary from culture to culture. When live-in relationships became legal, and so did the relationships in the LGBTQ community, these boundaries began to fade. When we accepted the fact that the LGBTQ community deserves the right to happiness and the right to live life like everyone else, we became more human. Once LGBTQ marriages started getting legal in different countries, the concept of family started taking different forms and began to evolve in a different direction.

Not just the LGBTQ but when many singles, divorced, and widow-widowers started feeling an intense need to be a family without being a part of the rigid marriage system; they started exploring the concept of family in new light.

What if any of them didn't have or want children but wanted a pet instead? Aren't they a family? What if two girls, who are singles and friends but not lesbians, decide to stay together, Aren't they a family?

The boundaries of relationships are fading day-by-day, blessing us with a broader mindset to look at humanity as a whole and not bound by names or culture or society.

This story of a gay is an eye-opener to change the perspective of the society towards the relationship of a man and a woman and same-gender relationships, while understanding sexual aspects of human life and going beyond. The story touches on different forms of love in different relations, sexual as well as platonic, and in combination with different genders throwing light on the possibility of a family system with no boundaries of sexual needs, gender, need of procreation, but the one that would be purely based on love and companionship.

1

Sameer

Hi, I am Sameer, a 30-year-old tall-fair-handsome, intelligent man with a multifaceted personality. I am not praising myself, but this is how others perceive me. Being an academically sound student throughout my career, I easily graduated as an IT engineer. In my last semester itself, I was picked up by a multinational company and got a super-paid job. I have finally settled down at an age at which my parents wanted me to. Yes, and to everyone's delight, I started with a family too!

Like each of us has, even I have a tale to tell, a tale that is very different from what we usually hear. It's the story of my life, and yes, it is about love too! It's a tale full of many tales. Whether it was a love story or not is completely up to you to decide.

Before I begin with my story, let me first give you a glimpse of my background. I belong to a typical middle-class Maharashtrian family in Pune. My father, an intelligent and committed man, retired as a general manager from a pharmaceutical company. This strong, aggressive, and overwhelming man over sixty, with a tall and broad physical frame, appears very intimidating even today. However, he has the softest heart in this world. I hold great respect for him, and the openness in our relationship makes him my ego-ideal.

Unlike my father, my mother has a very calm and composed demeanour. She has always won love from one and all around; she is a wonder woman. I share a deep bond with her even today. I have enjoyed doing everything with her, be it cooking, shopping, painting, or chitchatting during my childhood. I still like to spend time helping her with household work and support her in every possible way.

My parents have been far more broadminded and more supportive than most of my peers'. However, they brought me up in a very stereotypical background where the foundation of my mindset was set to 'the ideal'. I was groomed to be dutiful, obedient, truthful, and straightforward.

Being the only child of my parents, I was immensely loved. Naturally, my parents mean a lot to me. Meeting their expectations had always been a 'must-do' in my life; I not only met their expectations but exceeded them. I had always been 'the teacher's pet', 'a nerd' for my classmates, and 'the best son' for my parents. I was the topper of my class and was known as the 'award bagger' among the teachers. I was the chosen representative of my school for all inter-school competitions. Despite my achievements, I was a boy praised for my humbleness.

The aura of glory in school brought me envy. My jealous classmates mocked me and called me a 'book worm'. Even things that were genuinely worthy of appreciation became a subject of mockery. Their envious eyes found my sophisticated mannerisms and soft ways of expression 'girlish'. My sincerity and gentleness became the topic of their hurtful comments. I had grudges against them in my mind, and they had against me, but theirs grew to that extent that they boycotted me altogether. Gradually, I isolated myself from the groups in school and ended up being an introvert. Nevertheless, destiny did not spare me from pain. There was more to come to make my life rough and rugged.

2

Rough times

Even today, I believe that there is nothing wrong for a man to be interested in so-called 'women's stuff'. Someone's likes and dislikes have got nothing to do with their gender association. I have always had a genuine inclination towards cooking, pot painting, making jewellery, etc. However, one day my love for jewellery took a toll on me.

One Sunday, my mother and I visited a jewellery showroom. I was keenly observing the jewellery that my mother had bought. I was observing the gold earrings for a long time.

Looking at the mirror in my mother's hand, I asked, "May I try this, mom?"

Her angry expressions hushed me there itself, and I sadly put down the earrings back in the jewellery box. Unfortunately, a classmate of mine had come along with his parents to the same shop. When he was roaming here and there, trying to kill his boredom, he saw me picking up a pair of earrings passionately. I did not know that a thing as trivial as this would invite a nightmare the next day.

* * *

The next day, when I went to my classroom, I was surprised to find girls and boys whispering and giggling, looking at me. Confused with this weird behaviour, I went to my desk. The moment I saw my desk, I burst into tears. There was a picture drawn on my desk. It was a human whose lower body was of a male, and the upper half was of a female. On the top of the picture, they had written my name in capitals, 'SAMEER'. I felt very humiliated. I opened my water bottle, poured water on the desk, and wiped it off with my handkerchief. I wanted to avoid further embarrassment in front of my teacher; I felt like running away from the class. I sat on my bench and put my head down on the desk. I saw all boys and girls giggling, laughing, and ridiculing me. This was the worst ever feeling in my life.

The teacher came to the class a little late. The whole class stood up, and so did I, holding back my tears. I spent the day alone, suppressing my emotions without saying a word to anyone. I was waiting for the time to go home and cry out loud.

* * *

That evening when I stepped inside my house, I was on the verge of crying. Looking at my face, my mother came to me and gave me a warm hug. She kissed my cheek. Her warmth melted the frozen tears in my eyes. She asked, "What happened, dear? Why are you crying?"

Her single question burst the cloud of my pain. "Mumma..." I yelled with a cry and snuggled in her hug. I poured out my feelings. I narrated the entire story. She looked at me with eyes full of love and concern as she wiped my tears with her caring hands.

She said, "There is nothing wrong with your interest in jewellery. Even a jeweller is a man. Haven't you seen the sari vendors draping saris to show their customers? There is nothing wrong with doing that, Sameer. But society is narrow-minded when it comes to such things, so don't act this way. Boys are jealous of you because you are blessed with a good personality. Just ignore them and move on. Use their negative comments to excel positively in life. I will speak to your father today and ask him to complain about this incident to your class teacher. Be strong, my boy."

Her warm words consoled me and temporarily helped me dry my tears. However, something kept on bothering my mind though she was pretty convincing.

In the evening, my mother narrated the entire incident to my father. That night I sat beside my dad on my knees on the floor. Resting my arm on the arm of his chair, I leaned over him and asked, "Dad, do you think I am like a girl?"

My dad said, "No, my boy, you will become more like a man in the next few years. You have still not entered your teens. You are just a twelve year old. Just wait and watch... you will be the most handsome man in your batch. Half the boys in your class don't even have a trace of a beard or a moustache. So why think about it? Even my classmates used to tease me as I got my beard late."

That made perfect sense and silenced my worried mind chatter. Many more times I was teased, harassed, but I faced it all with great strength. I wept, I cried, I was hurt, I was frustrated, but I never gave up. I fought with courage. I faced such ups and downs with great positivity till then. I focussed my effort on making my parents and teachers proud. But things changed as I entered my teenage as 'nothing lasts long', and so did this phase of my life.

3

Confronting my reflection

It was an early morning, my usual newspaper reading time. The smell of the early morning fresh air was making me feel lively. I was reading a newspaper with a cup of milk in my bedroom. After going through all headlines and important news, I flipped through 'page 3'. My cursory eyes running across the page caught a large picture of a hot model. He was shirtless, showing off his 8-pack abs with low-waist jeans fitting well on his irresistible masculine body. The moment I saw him, my awestruck mouth opened into a big 'Oh my God'. As my eyes went down his chest, it turned me on. I felt a sensation of hotness all over my body, my face, and my ears. I could not control my urge to kiss the picture. I placed my lips over his photo and rubbed my penis. The feeling intensified so much that I unknotted my pyjamas and began stroking my penis. I was fumbling in the beginning, but later I reached a climax and ejaculated for the first time in my life.

It was my very first deliberate encounter with my sexuality at the tender age of twelve. I looked in the mirror with a sense of discomfort and guilt. I was terribly mad and uncomfortable with the wetness in my pants and the stickiness on my hands. The 'first-time ejaculation shock' did not trouble me much, but the fact that it was because of a man did. When I looked in the mirror, my forehead was wet with sweat. The wetness under my pants was scaring me even more than the sweat on my forehead. My head had started spinning in the whirlpool of infinite thoughts in my mind.

I knew this was not normal. It was not what happened to everyone. I was different from others. I felt something had killed the 'good boy' in me. 'Why me?' I thought. When I was so perfect in every possible way, why had this happened to me? When I was the 'ideal' son for parents, the 'best student' for my teachers, why this imperfection had to destroy my life? Why this big blow had to haunt my naïve and innocent mind? This one blemish was going to ruin my self-image. Why was I abnormal? Well, was it really abnormal? I was thinking about it again and again.

I suddenly remembered an incident during our English class. While reading aloud a poem in an English textbook, we had come across the word 'gay'. Everyone had started giggling at that time. I did not know what it was. So, when I had checked it out in the dictionary, I clearly had understood that there existed men who felt attraction for men. A few months later, the same curiosity had stopped my eyes on the 'ask the Sexpert' column of the Times of India. The column answered a concern faced by gay. That was the time I understood that this thing existed and was scientifically considered natural.

But I had never imagined that something like that would ever happen to me. But why it had to be with me when I had a perfect life till now? It was difficult, very difficult for me to accept this fact. I was dying with this guilt and with the feeling that no one was like me. I had no one to share these feelings, and the pressure of digesting it all alone made things even more difficult.

4

The inner struggle

I tried to swallow the fact with a pinch of salt. But the more I tried, the more I felt like proving that I was like everyone else. I wondered, what if my parents had not stopped me from interacting with girls? Perhaps I wouldn't have been this way. So I decided to try it out. I wanted to see what would happen if I got closer to girls; spoke with them the way other boys did. I wanted to try all possible ways to feel perfect again.

The next day I smiled at the most beautiful girl in our class. Her name was Mohini. I purposely borrowed a notebook from her telling her that I wanted to complete my homework. She lent it to me. My fingers touched hers while taking the book, but I felt nothing. But I did not give it up.

We had a gorgeous teacher who taught us history. Many boys in our class had a crush on her. I tried to observe her during the class. I secretly stared at her tummy, which was partially visible from her transparent, well-draped sari. But it had no effect on me as I felt a motherly feeling towards her. I was frustrated by then and felt repulsed.

That was the very first time I had gotten rid of the inhibitions on my thoughts and set them to run free. But every time I tried thinking about the most beautiful and the hottest girl or woman, I ended up feeling nothing.

However, during this process of letting go of my emotions, I understood that I did like some boys physically. I also felt intense feelings of adoration for some. I was a boy who adored people for their intellectual qualities and never looks. So, whenever I liked a guy, I felt that I liked him for his virtues like intelligence or attributes of nature as sexual feelings did not come to my mind then. I mistook them for feelings of friendship and ignored them. Sometimes I even felt like kissing a boy on the cheek or giving him a tight hug. Thinking retrospectively, the picture was very clear. I had always been gay.

I could see my life in a different colour which was certainly not pleasant. I knew I was made that way. I also realised why the boys in my class ridiculed me. It was not entirely out of jealousy but a form of ragging. They suspected, or rather, were sure I was 'gay'. I often felt like sharing this with someone but had no one to talk to me about this. Being a sincere devotee of the Almighty, I started visiting Lord Hanuman's temple. I tried to empty my heart to the Lord and prayed to him to make me like everyone else. I asked God several times if he was punishing me for some mistakes I made in the past. However, despite my sincere prayers, he did not change me into a straight man. As I had never done a bad thing in my life, I felt there was no reason for him to punish me. So I understood that it was his wish and decided to accept the fact.

This fact came upon me like a blow, completely destroying my innocence. It filled my life with loneliness and negativity. I was still not able to accept the fact that I was not like everyone else. But every time I tried to be like others, reality hit me hard. But to my surprise, a new chapter in my life was waiting to tell me that I was not alone!

5

The gay gang

"Mirror mirror on the wall,
Am I good enough so that for me, someone would fall?"

During my frequent tries to feel attracted toward girls, I had noticed that some girls in my class had a crush on me. I was good looking enough to impress any girl. Well, but I was looking out for boys and not girls.

When the 'birds and bees' talks begun to buzz, excitement was in the air. School life was so happening now. Either someone was caught writing a love letter, or someone was caught staring at someone. Just like others, I had started exploring my years of puberty too. Even I had developed a couple of crushes on my seniors.

When I saw other boys and girls having a crush on each other, even I felt that someone should care for me, adore me, and love me the way they loved one another. But I had no single person around me even to share this emotion.

However, destiny was not so unfair. The annual gathering brought some light to my dark life. Students from eighth to tenth class were to perform two skits similar to street plays, where a few actors did multiple roles. As most of the roles were of boys, our teacher decided to make it an 'all-boys' skit. A few female roles in the skit were to be done by the boys. The class teachers of the three classes announced that they would award the boys who will play female roles, and four boys raised their hands. I was one of them. I was very good at acting and especially acting in a female role.

Our practice sessions started, and I met the three other boys who were playing female roles. There was something familiar amongst us.

One day after our practice session, we were chitchatting about other boys in the skit. Akash said, "Mihir acts so good. I think he has done an acting workshop!"

"Oh, that's right, but his built is even more striking. Have you ever seen a boy of our age having such a muscular built?" Akash bubbled.

Pranit said, "Oh come on, Akash, I find Arun far better than him. He is tall and handsome. How irresistible he is!"

This reaction was bizarre coming from a boy. Pranit and Akash were friends as they travelled by the same school bus.

"I disagree, my friends. I find Mihir better. I feel so jealous of Ria. Mihir likes her so much," Vivek said with a conspicuous wink.

At that instant, I quickly and shyly smiled and said, "I like Nitin. He is a cutie pie." All of them gave naughty smiles, and we all understood what we had to.

This incident revealed to me how gays explored other men to confirm whether the other man was gay or not. We hardly spoke about any actresses. Our conversations revolved only around male actors and models. Along with that, girlish ways of behaviour, expressions, gait, and how men spoke gave more clues. This was the way I understood men found out who are gays.

As we grew closer, we found out that each of us had faced ragging at some point in our lives because of our different gender or sexual orientation. But now we had that feeling soothing our hearts, *'we are not alone'*. Vivek, Akash, Pranit and I became friends forever. I was in eighth standard, Vivek and Akash were in tenth, and Pranit in ninth. We never felt any attraction for one another though we were gays. We shared a brotherly bond. The best phase of my life had begun. You must have found this an unrealistic and unbelievable coincidence, but I was lucky to find such gay friends in my school itself.

I developed my first crush during that time. In the skit, I played the role of Nitin's wife. Nitin was in class tenth. The moment my eyes had fallen on him, I had felt drawn towards him. I had that 'love at first sight feeling' for him. He was my type, taller than me, with a broad chest, dark glowing complexion, and broad shoulders. Every time he stood near me in the act, my excitement knew no bounds. Every time he touched me for some act, I felt like kissing his lips. I enjoyed smelling his perfume on my shirt. I was on the top of the world to get a chance to play his wife.

Though I knew he liked a girl, I fantasised about sitting with him on a seashore in an embrace. Every night I used to think about him. I loved imagining us studying together, going to the library, and sharing notes. This was the first time in my life that I had developed tender feelings for a boy. The joy of sharing these feelings was even greater than having them. I felt very lucky to have new friends to talk to about it. My friends teased me playfully every time he came close to me during the rehearsals. They tickled and poked me, and we had fun like never in life. Just like me, the secret compartments of everyone's hearts were unlocked. My teenage had taken a new turn. With every practice session, we got closer, and the bond we shared grew stronger. We all had become known as 'the gang of girls'. But none of us really cared anymore as we were not alone. The old wounds of ragging seemed to be dressed now. From this phase of our life till today, all of us are still good friends. Time and distance have distanced us, but our hearts connect at any moment.

6

School is over

After my annual gathering ended, I did not realise when my annual exams had begun and now were on the verge of getting over. After finding such close friends, I did not realise how my life had taken the speed of light. From that year, my life stopped moving and began to fly!

I finished my last paper, and my summer vacation started. I loved summers, loved the pleasant nights after the hot and dry days, and enjoyed the mangoes, the melons, and the coconut water. My birthday fell in May and so in the summer vacation. Until this year, I never had friends, so I preferred celebrating my birthday with my family. But this birthday was going to be special with my newly found friends. For the first time in my life, I was going to invite friends to my place.

My summer vacations were full of fun and play. I loved playing hide and seek and cricket during the day. In the night, I tried new recipes for my mom and dad. Every summer, my cousins gathered at my place. Summertime was for family and now for my friends too!

From this summer onwards, my vacations were going to be different. My gang and I had plans! We good boys were going to open our dirty compartments during this vacation! We had never done that with other boys before. Akash had managed to get a collection of 'Faa', a magazine that always had pictures of hot models and articles on bold topics. We had plans to read novels on gay life and watch pornographic films in cyber cafes even though it was prohibited. We were going to do things that we had never done and were going to enjoy to the fullest.

The advent of summers had set my mind free from all the restrictions. Finding this new, small world with my friends had liberated me, giving me strong wings to take a free flight to my teenage.

7

Naughty times

My vacation fun time started with Pranit, Akash, and Vivek. It was not going to be very long that they would be in their colleges. So I wanted to cherish every precious moment of us together. We all were in high spirits. Vivek's brother was a couple of years older, so he had a few gay novels. His brother had no clue why we were so interested in exploring the gay love life. We read those novels during the afternoon at his place when his parents were out for work and his brother in his college. He read out these books, adding a lot of drama to them with powerful intonations. We enjoyed listening to him. He was the reader of our gang. When he read the description of lovemaking for the first time, my hair stood on its end. Akash and Vivek were very much used to such things as they had greater exposure. This was the first time I had known something about gay lovemaking.

The other day we planned to watch pornographic films. It wasn't easy to get stuff like porn those days. Though this was illegal and risky, we found it adventurous. We went to a cybercafé where we could watch such films at ₹20 per hour. In school days, it was very difficult getting even such a small amount of money from parents. We had to lie for the same. It was the first time I lied to my parents. I wasn't used to such behaviour before. My parents were very particular in asking the details about my expenditure. So, I had told them that we go to parks and hang out spots in Pune to eat bhelpuri. That was convincing enough because they knew I loved '*chaat*'.

That was the first time I watched such a film in my life. We had no guts to ask the cybercafé guy to give us gay porn. We were scared that people might find out that we were gays. All we could enjoy was seeing the nude men. People around thought we came here to see straight porn, but we had to quench our thirst by seeing a man nude. Though that time we found this phase of life very exciting and adventurous, today I realise how difficult it had been for us since then. We had to extract joy from things that were never natural to others.

One fine day, it was Akash's birthday. So, we went to 'Rupali', a famous restaurant in Pune where he was going to give us a treat. There we saw a very hot man, tall, with long hair, with a slim built, dressed in a sleeveless t-shirt and faded jeans that hung very low on his waist. We kept stalking him for a couple of hours. The day got full of life when we could see someone with looks as wild as his.

Retrospectively, today I realise how difficult it was for us even to find options for dating then and even later. It was difficult to flirt with the preferred gender the way boys of our age did. But at that point of time, we were delighted as we, the birds of the same flock, could at least share our happiness and sorrows.

It was fun to do such adventures when our parents believed that 'these good boys will never do the forbidden'. But we all wondered what if they ever find out that our gender itself was 'the forbidden'.

8

Summer air

My cousin brothers were going to visit my place for around ten days. We all shared such a wonderful bond that the age differences made no difference in our love. We maternal cousins had been having play dates together even since we were in diapers. As we grew up and started going to schools, our summer get-togethers started. As we had a spacious big house, the reunions were always planned at our place. We enjoyed playing around the house and sleeping under the starlit sky on the terrace. Sometimes even my mother and father joined us. If my aunts and uncles were also there, it was a great family reunion. We sung songs, played games, and listened to horror tales at night. As it was a 'cousins only' get together, it meant playing and playing all day long. Parag, Ritwik, Pinakin, and Lalit were lovely company. Parag and Pinakin were two years younger than me, and Ritwik and Lalit were three years younger. This year, Tanmay my eldest cousin brother, was also going to join us. He was five years older than me. Tanmay had stayed in the US for the last five years. His parents had come back to India forever this year.

Tanmay was in the process of getting enrolled in the first year of his BBA.

I had met him three years back. I had adored Tanmay a lot when I had met him last time. He was super intelligent and witty. Whenever it came to games or petty fights with my cousins, it was Tanmay who always took my side. I was eagerly looking forward to meeting him.

So, on the third day of my vacation, all my cousins arrived except Tanmay. My US returned brother was going to join us the next day. My mom and dad had grand plans for his welcome, and we cousins were excited to hear his 'foreign' special stories. We were going to listen to stories about his school, his friends, 'the whys and hows' in the US and how things are different there. We all were proud of him and were looking forward to meeting him.

9

Summer secrets

My cousins had arrived, and their chitter-chatter added enthusiasm to the holiday mood. The blow of being gay had destroyed my innocence at a very young age. So being in company with my younger innocent cousins brought back the child in me.

Early in the morning, the doorbell rang, and Tanmay came to our place with an air of celebrity. The whole house seemed to be lit up with his presence. His cheerful expressions and dynamic demeanour impressed everyone. All of us brothers were full of awe and respect for him. I was wondering whether he would treat me differently or would still have the same soft corner. But to my surprise, we both hardly took any time to gel well once again. Time had not faded the bond we shared. In fact, as I had grown up we had more things to share with each other, and perhaps I thought more was waiting for me in the future.

After listening to Tanmay's stories and relishing my mom-made cuisines the whole day, we all were excited for sky gazing in the night. We laid down mattresses on the terrace. Tanmay carried one stack, and I carried another. When we went upstairs, Tanmay laid the first two and said, "Sameer, we are big boys, so we will sleep in the end and keep a watch on kids, okay?" I obediently nodded. I was so overjoyed to know he did not consider me as a kid anymore. I always liked 'us', being addressed as a team. It brought an ear to ear smile to my face.

It was a fine, dark night. We finished our dinner and gathered on the terrace for the most awaited time of the day. My father showed us the moon and the stars. I always enjoyed this family ritual of sky gazing during summertime.

After an hour, we started feeling sleepy and decided to wind up. Tanmay and my father carried the telescope downstairs. When they came up, we were sleeping in a row. My father turned around and said, "Tanmay, you have great leadership qualities. From the last two years, none of these young boys had slept in a row on the terrace. They usually mess up the mattresses like pigs on the farm. You have disciplined them so well." He laughed and walked downstairs, humming some tune. I felt so proud of Tanmay and felt glad that he considered me worthy of his friendship.

* * *

It was 2 a.m. in the night. I was fast asleep but was woken up by discomfort and some weird feeling. I thought it was some dream. When I felt more conscious, I found what I had been feeling or seeing was not a dream at all. There was someone's hand touching me under the blanket, trying to unknot my pants. The shock woke me up. At that moment, I was sure that what I saw was no dream but a reality. I felt terrified when I understood that it was none other than Tanmay's hand.

Tanmay immediately understood that I was about to scream with fear. He quickly forced shut my mouth tight with his hand. It wasn't like I did not understand what was going on. I had recently seen some videos of gay lovemaking. But this coming from my brother shook me in and out. I was shocked by the unexpected. I had never imagined that this could happen to me. I was motionless with a jolt of this unexpected situation.

When I felt his hand caressing and teasing my private parts, I was motionless with fear. In the very beginning, I felt repulsed. But slowly, as he did not stop and continued exploring my body, I started feeling better. He undid the knot of my pants, and his hand found its way to my penis. The stress built in me found a vent, and I started feeling high. I felt something that was deeply suppressed in me began to sublime. I had neither expected that I would allow this, nor I had ever imagined that I could enjoy this. I reached the climax at a point, and yes, I got the same pleasure that every man gets. Though I was bitten by this sudden behaviour of my brother, I secretly found a thrill in every moment.

That bright night I got the most treasurable experience in my life. The cold breeze blew on my face, and my heart felt very contented. The doubt that I will never find someone who will love me had vanished. Now I knew that yes, there was someone who felt I was good enough. I knew I was good. Even the girls liked me. I knew it very well. But that wasn't important. I wanted a man with whom I will fall in love. It was difficult to find a partner in a limited pool of gays. So, though he was my brother, my heart convinced my thoughts to keep the brotherhood aside and think of him as a lover. I had never thought he liked me this way, but I was glad I had found someone really dashing and adventurous.

My heart raced and ran, leaving a scarlet red blush on my face. Till the day before, I had never ever thought that someone would like me physically too. That night, I felt like I was so complete. I was too young for all of this. But, at the same time, I felt accepted, I felt appreciated and, more importantly, 'his'.

After the 'secret activity', neither he nor I spoke a word. I wanted to look into his eyes and enjoy the feeling of being his. But he turned his back towards me and slept. I kept on looking at his back in the moonlight. I could hear him snore lightly. I did the same, assuming even he must be feeling shy after this bold move. I kept on reliving the moment the whole night and did not realise when I fell asleep.

10

A morning so different

The next morning, I was woken up with the kiss of warm sunrays. I had been sleeping for a long time. I could hear everyone calling me. Then came the final call by my mother, accompanied by the aroma of breakfast, opened my sleepy eyes. My head felt heavy, and suddenly the scenes of last night flashed in front of my eyes, opening them even wider. I immediately checked my left side, where Tanmay had been sleeping. But all the mattresses were neatly folded and stacked up in the corner of the terrace. There was no trace of Tanmay and even my younger cousins.

"Sameer... you are late... come soon... we all are waiting for you... come soon." There were more calls. How I wished it would have been Tanmay's hand on my forehead, waking me up lovingly. But that was not practical at all. It was a secret and was going to remain a secret forever. Unlike today, gay love was taboo and a sin. It was just that I was happy it had happened to me, and at least it served as a memory to spend my life alone or perhaps with him.

With a sheepish smile on my face, I descended the staircase with a pounding heart. The moment

I entered the kitchen, my eyes stopped on Tanmay. For the first time in my life, I had thought of someone as 'my prince charming'. I observed his face in the new light of love. I found his chubby face so adorable. The sweat on his nose, above his thin lips and his chubby cheeks overloaded him with cuteness. His lips opened up like a bow flashing up a smile casting a spell on me. His hair set well as the hair gel gave him a hot look. Usually, I liked slim and strong men. I wondered what attracted me to him. He was a chubby boy, but for me, he looked cute, like a teddy bear, fluffy and soft. I felt like hugging him at that moment. I kept staring at his lips as he took a bite of the hot *idli* my mother served. When I looked at him intently, I felt a jolt of special feeling through me. My tummy took a nosedive, and I immediately looked away, feeling embarrassed. Tanmay had noticed me gawking at him, but he turned his eyes towards my father and continued his discussion on the India Pakistan cricket match. Well, that was bound to happen. After all, how could he be open about our relationship? We had to act like brothers in front of everyone. I always wondered how he had managed to find out my sexual orientation. Anyway, I have never found an answer to this riddle even today!

This morning was very special to me. I had expected that, like other boys in our class, even Tanmay would give me a love letter or maybe a quick kiss. But nothing of that sort ever happened. The whole day I found his behaviour so normal that I could not believe it was he who had done it last night. His usual gesture, 'hey bro', that once I found very cool, now killed me every moment. I wished he stopped doing that. Perhaps he did that purposely to hide it from others, I thought. How

I wished, instead of wearing this mask of brotherhood, he would express his feelings to me.

But I knew I had to go through this pain if I wanted his love. For my heart knew he loved me too. The whole day his presence warmed up my face. My heart was beating faster than ever. I kept on waiting for that one moment when he would say 'I love you', but nothing of that sort happened. My mind had become a pendulum oscillating between the extremes of excitement and disillusionment. As the night approached, the excitement and the nervousness of my heart reached the peak. I wasn't sure what was going to happen. But I hoped that before doing anything, at least he will give his first signal of love.

That night Tanmay repeated the same thing. It was not easy to do it when all the cousins were sleeping in a row. There was a huge risk involved. Anybody would have woken up and could have spotted us. Though it was night and a few streetlights glowed in the dark, the sky was enough lit up with stars to affect privacy. Tanmay was brilliant and had solutions to every problem. He had laid down our mattresses very smartly. He kept some distance between my mattress and the mattress of the cousin next to me, taking advantage of the dent on the terrace floor. He also chose dark and longer blankets for us.

Well, all this meant staying very quiet and making no sound. I had decided to cooperate with him as much as I could. Though he had expressed nothing verbally, I had assumed this act as a sign of mute love. So, I wanted to help him take this initiative in all possible ways. I was more excited and more aroused. A transparent thread of secret understanding was woven between us.

I knew by now that he loved me, and I was scared of losing him. So, I preferred not to force him to express anything verbally. However, I was very immature then and kept assuming this expression of 'lust' as love. The whole episode of last night happened again. But this night, I felt more liberated. I had managed to let go of my inhibitions and lived it up.

After some time, Tanmay slept. How much ever I tried to sleep, I could not. The guilt of rejoicing romance was pinching my heart. I found myself questioning my morals every minute. But the next moment, I found myself justifying my act. '*Though he was my brother, at least I knew him, and I shared a good connection with him. It was better to be with someone you connect well and already share a good bond with rather than living alone. How did being a brother matter anyway? In India, marriages of cousin brothers and sisters weren't uncommon. I convinced my mind that the man I had fallen for had special feelings for me. How did that even matter that he was my brother?*' My arguments with myself continued for hours together. My tired, sleepy mind tamed my devil's advocate, silencing my mental chatter, and I fell asleep at dawn.

11

The frozen conversation

Nights were bright, and days were dark. The whole vacation, I knitted stories from Tanmay's gestures and tried to establish some meaning to justify his behaviour. Though I was lost in my own dream world, the guilt of getting into such a physically intimate relationship was still bothering me intermittently. I was prepared for an emotional relationship but not a physical one. I belonged to a school of thought that all these things are not right at such a young age and, moreover, not justified, at least until a long-term commitment. But the spell he had cast on me stopped all these thoughts.

My days passed in the thoughts of night, and the nights passed under Tanmay's hypnotic spell. I was caught in the emotional tornado haunting me day and night. The vacation time flew fast, and the day of Tanmay's departure to Mumbai arrived. He had to go back to begin with his enrolling procedures and other formalities. The other cousins were to stay for another week. I felt depressed and sad. Despite getting many opportunities, Tanmay had not confessed his feelings. I yearned for those three words. But I knew the time was running out, and I would not get what I wanted.

It was hard to accept that he was going to go, and I will never hear those three words. But I was still not convinced. So, I determined to give it a last try. If he had decided not to speak out, I had to.

All my cousins were busy getting ready. Taking advantage of the privacy, I called Tanmay in the kitchen. I tried to hold his hand and pull him closer to say something, but at the very moment, he hushed me with a finger on my lips and said, "Keep it a secret," and quickly left.

The conversation froze there itself, and my eyes were in tears. I wanted to ask him how we were going to talk. Was he okay with a telephone call or a letter? I wanted to ask him. But the moment I tried to follow him to the living room, my father rushed with Tanmay's luggage and said, "My boy, be quick. It's time to catch the bus. Ask Tanmay if he is ready." I swallowed those unspoken words that did not reach Tanmay's heart and did as I was told. There was a lot of chatter while saying goodbye. My father asked if I wanted to come to drop him at the bus station, but I avoided it to hide the tears that wetted my silent eyes. My wet eyes could not see him disappear as my frozen unspoken words dissolved in the sad silence.

12

Sameer so different

My missing fever subsided within a couple of days. What remained was romanticism and memories of the vacation. There was a sudden change in my life. My life was now more colourful than ever. I had suddenly become conscious about the way I looked, spoke, and behaved. Till now, I never looked in the mirror except for important occasions, but now I hardly missed a single chance to do so. Though Tanmay's departure was painful, I started feeling very different after he left. I fell in love with myself for the first time in my life, just the way I was also in love with him. Every day, whenever I went out or even when I was at home, I was very much presentable. I was more particular in maintaining my hairstyle and became more interested in picking up good outfits for myself.

Every time I looked at my reflection, I felt as if Tanmay's eyes were gazing at me. That feeling had transformed me into someone different. My life was drenched in the seven colours of the rainbow, and I bathed in its beauty. Life was so rose glassed now. I had started noticing beauty in every silly thing around me. I felt blessed and felt that Tanmay was the best gift given by God to me. I successfully hid the special feelings from my family, but at some corner of my heart, I felt like sharing this with my friends at the earliest. I was super excited and was waiting for the right moment.

After all my brothers had left, I planned a meet up with my gang. It was more of a small group than a gang, but calling it a gang underlined the strength of our unity. All of us met at Akash's home, which had a beautiful garden. His house was small and cosy. Whenever there was no one at home, we enjoyed complete freedom.

Once Vivek and Pranit had gathered, the secret hiding inside my tummy started wobbling to come out. Akash looked at me from head to toe. He had never seen me so well dressed. He looked at me and asked, narrowing his eyes, "Are you going out to have dinner today?" I nodded to say no. Akash was even more surprised and tried to poke me, "How come you are wearing such well-ironed clothes today? For a change, your trousers are in the right combination with your t-shirt. Usually, you don't even think about the colour of your clothes, do you? I won't be surprised if you wear a white t-shirt on white trousers."

Everyone laughed...

He sarcastically added further, "When I wear good clothes, you asked me if I was wearing them to impress someone. Now, who is the reason behind this great change in you?"

I felt embarrassed, and I blushed, trying to hide my smile. In fact, this was the moment I had been waiting for. I wanted to share with them every little thing in my life.

"Well... I have someone in my life... I am in love. It happened during my vacations."

"Oh! Look! In the world where straight people are single, this lucky boy has got a boyfriend!" said Vivek.

For a moment, the word boyfriend reminded me that he had not said those three words to me yet. I overcame the wave of sadness suppressing my excitement and went on. But I hid the fact and said, "My cousin, Tanmay..." There went my story, and my friends were amazed.

"Ah, the boy you introduced us to during the birthday party..." asked Akash.

"Yes," I replied.

From that day, my friends started teasing me. Every time they mentioned him, butterflies fluttered in my stomach. This teasing was good enough to wipe off my tears of missing and make me smile more. The hot summer days rolled away, and it was time to go back to school.

It was the very first time when I went to school feeling more confident and attractive than ever. Nothing mattered to me more than Tanmay did. Now my life had taken a new turn. My hard work and my efforts in life were dedicated only to impress him. My career to prove I was worthy was only to make him mine for my entire life. It was because of him my life had become more meaningful.

13
A ray of hope

After Tanmay left, I had always been thinking to find out how I can establish frequent communication with him. This was not an over expectation because I had heard couples doing the same. This silence was getting more and more intolerable. I had realised that he was shy to take initiatives practically. But I was very good at it, so why not keep trying? During those days, mobiles were not very common, and the net packs not so cheap. The mobiles that middle-class people used had limited features. Smartphones were not very common and, at least, not amongst schoolboys. Neither WhatsApp nor a cheap video calling facility was readily available. So, communicating with our loved ones was not very convenient. It had been ages, and I had not spoken to Tanmay. But as time passed, it was difficult for me to resist doing so. Every now and then, I kept thinking about ways to speak to him, come what may! One day, I determined to make it happen.

Why in the world would anyone stop a boy from speaking to his cousin brother? My parents had no idea about my sexual orientation. My parents wouldn't have thought about it even in one of their nightmares. I found out a silly reason to speak to him.

One day when I returned from my school, I asked my father, "Dad, from this year we have to do projects to improve our application-oriented understanding in Science. I want to consult Tanmay regarding a project I am planning to work on. He had worked on a similar topic, so can I call him? I thought he would be some help to me. What do you think?" My guilt had stupefied me to a level that I did not realise I was asking my father's permission for a thing I had been doing without asking anyone ever in my life.

Dad looked surprised and said, "Are you alright? Why are you asking me that? Is it an indirect way of seeking help from me for the project and gave a naughty smile?" His brown eyes twinkled. He always did that when I tried to seek any indirect help from him. But this time, the story was different. I gasped in my mind, '*Thank God... he had misunderstood the hidden agenda.*' My dad was smart enough to understand that something was fishy. After all, he knew me so well. Had he known of me being gay, he would have definitely understood this too.

I decided to let him stay in the same impression. I quickly cleared things as if I were caught. "Well... Dad... yes... I do need some help from you as there is a deadline. I will be very happy if you help me."

"Caught you, my son... don't forget I am your father," said my dad triumphantly. I saw him laughing and heaved a sigh of relief.

"I will speak with you once I discuss the topic with Tanmay." I said while fidgeting with my fingers. It was worth lying for the second time, and I had lied well.

My hands had become wet with nervousness as I approached the telephone. I felt so excited that I was going to hear his manly, husky voice after a long time. My heart thumped with excitement, and I was already head over heels. The phone rang, and my heart started singing and dancing at the end of the last ring.

"Hello, who is this?" Tanmay's voice soothed my ears. After a long pause, I spoke in a very low confident way, "Hi! Tanmay, it's... it's me, Sameer. I fell short of words. "Aaa... I... I wanted some help from you... mm... can we talk?" "Hi bro... how have you been?" Tanmay's words hit me like a hammer; I hated them. "Yes," I politely replied, "I am good. How are you? Tanmay, I needed your help. "Yes, please, tell me. I would be happy to help you. Hope uncle and aunty are doing well and you are too. Yes, I will be happy to help you anytime. Tell me, what do you want me to do?"

We spoke about the project for twenty minutes, but it seemed like two for me. The conversation revolved around the project and nothing personal. After we had finished talking about it, my voice lowered suddenly. I gathered courage and asked, "Tanmay, do you miss me? I miss you every night. I think of you during..." Before I could speak further, Tanmay interrupted my talk and changed the topic. He said, "So which new car did uncle buy and what colour is it?" I tried to answer something. Then he extended the conversation jumping to another topic. "How is your school? I hope all is well! Do call me if you need anything. You are always welcome. Bye, see you... I have got to go."

One more time, my words were not heard before I swallowed those unheard emotions. I was deeply disheartened. Well, I could understand; maybe uncle aunty might have been around. After all, he had asked me to keep this a secret. I pondered a lot. Then it dawned on me, *'call me if you need anything'* was a signal he wanted to give me that he would always be there for me at any point time.

I loved my habit of analysing things. It did help me to understand the hidden meanings. Every time I remembered those words, I felt better. But this state did not last for long. He had spoken to me for quite a long time, and that still bothered me every now and then.

But the good part was, I had got the golden key to the door of my love. My project was to continue for another four months till I appeared for my annual exams of class 9th. So, till then, I had an all-time reason to speak with Tanmay. I started calling him every weekend. Most of the times, Tanmay answered his call, but sometimes he did not. Whenever he answered the call, the conversations were always very friendly and focused on studies. We spoke about everything under the sun but not about us. When I tried to speak about other things, they majorly revolved around our families. However, whenever I tried to drive the topic to us or our relationship, he remained cold. Despite my repeated attempts to pull Tanmay into a romantic, lovey-dovey conversation, Tanmay did not budge. He never spoke to me like a boyfriend. But I tried to be more understanding and blamed this behaviour on the social conditions and family pressure. I also accepted the fact that Tanmay will continue to behave in the same way on the phone. However, a tiny flame of hope flickered in my heart that once we meet, things will fall in place. I had to wait with patience during this long, tough time, for it was the test of my true love.

14

Waiting for him

The project related calls with Tanmay helped me sustain the parting pain. The lame support of infrequent and emotionless calls kindled my hope to make him mine. I was badly waiting for the summer vacation and Tanmay's arrival. But the annual exams were yet to get over.

I had worked very hard this year. It was the very first time I had faced a serious distraction in my life. I had not imagined how it was going to affect my academics. I had to ensure that my emotional state would not reflect on my progress card. It was an enormous challenge.

My teacher disclosed last week that my name had been nominated for the 'The Star Student Award of the Year'. My academic excellence and success in the science fair had paid me off this time. So, I was eagerly waiting for Tanmay to come and see with his own eyes me being conferred with that honour. This was going to shut the mouths of those who mocked me for being gay. My heart had already started pounding with excitement. I was sure that getting this award was going to make Tanmay feel proud of me.

My daydreaming helped the time pass with a greater speed. The hope that things might get better this time had given me tremendous zest. As the date of his arrival was nearer, bells had started jingling in my mind. The garden of my heart was blooming with the fresh flowers of Tanmay's thoughts.

After I finished with my last written exam, I kept on thinking of ways to woe Tanmay. I was not going to leave a single stone unturned to impress him. I was going to do a makeover. I had pre-planned a haircut secretly. I also asked my mother to gift me my birthday jeans and t-shirt earlier so that I can wear them when we all go out for dinner. I wanted to show him that now I was grown up and no longer that 'kiddish' Sameer. I had tried reading a few books on love and romance to develop my lovemaking skills. Maybe I thought he felt I was too young for a real relationship. I just wanted to convince him somehow that he should find his future partner in me. I was a staunch believer of one principle 'if you take efforts in the right direction, no one could stop you from getting what you wanted'. So, my sincere love was not going to go unrequited. I just had to wait for the right time to come.

15

One more time

My cousins had arrived, and Tanmay was expected in another couple of hours. Amidst the hustle and bustle at home, I was feeling very lonely without him. I was dressed in my best clothes, desperately waiting to welcome Tanmay. I had heard him tell one of my cousins that he liked green. I had specially ironed a parrot green shirt and wore it on the brown-coloured trousers. My hair was freshly cut, and I flaunted my new haircut. The clock ticked slowly. I was getting restless with every minute. The pressure of nervousness was building up in my heart, making me slightly breathless.

The doorbell rang, and there he was. My younger brothers yelled out with excitement, "It's Tanmay Dada (brother)." The youngest of all, Pinakin, crazily hopped and rushed to open the door. I felt too shy to face Tanmay, so I stayed back. I hid behind the pillar on which an old landscape hung. It was the most inconspicuous place in the entire living room. I felt a little more secure there as I was not easily visible. I was very conscious of his presence and was struggling to come out of the tunnel of nervousness.

I was cautious about my facial expressions. I did not want my nervousness to be visible. I tried to mask it with excitement. I was desperately waiting to see Tanmay's reaction when his eyes would notice me. As Tanmay entered the house, I felt a cool breeze comforting me. A spontaneous smile spread across my face. Before I could realise, my eyes started glittering with joy, and my body warmed up with his presence.

His dynamic persona shone bright with the spark of his intelligence despite his average looks. He wore a funky t-shirt with trousers that perfectly matched it. My eyes could not leave his tanned face, which was now covered with stubbles, and my mouth was agape, mesmerised by his presence.

He walked towards me after exchanging words of regards with my mother and father. He patted gently on the back of other brothers in his usual way of saying hello to younger ones. Absentmindedly I kept on looking at my feet to hide my nervousness, and, 'Thud', Tanmay hit my back with his strong hands. "Where are you lost, man?" and I looked at him coyly, smiling back. I could notice the way he hit my back. It sent a wave of excitement through my body. So unexpected and yet so aggressively exciting. The sudden bang on my back sent an electrical jolt through my heart too.

"It's time for lunch, my boys. Take your plates and sit on the dining table," called my mother. "Tanmay, we all are hungry, be quick, freshen up and join us. You all can chitchat later." The kitchen smelt of different cuisines. Her call for lunch and the smells from the kitchen brought this foodie back to the present. I was used to spending a very long time in my dream world. Many times, I was shaken or pinched back to the real world by someone. My parents had already started calling me Mr absentminded. Even teachers had asked me to stand up in the class whenever they found me lost in my own world.

Waking up from my dream world, I went into the kitchen. I saw Tanmay helping my mother serve food. Being born and brought up in the US, he had learnt to be self-dependent and was used to cooking and other household stuff, unlike Indian boys. I admired him for this. There was so much to learn from him.

We all took our seats. My father and mother sat at the positions of the hosts, opposite each other. Tanmay, in no time, took a vacant seat beside me. I had not at all expected that he would occupy a chair which was beside me. As he sat, his arm brushed mine. My cheeks were scarlet red with his touch. I lowered my head to hide my face and kept looking at the plate below. I did not speak with anyone while eating. My mother asked me while serving a Chapatti, "What's wrong with you, Sameer? Why aren't you speaking with anyone?" I could not control my smile. I looked upward and said, smiling wide, "No, mom, I am super hungry. I am savouring your delicious food. I am giving justice to it," I said while gobbling up. My mom smiled in return and turned to Ritwik. "Today, you all will get to taste Sameer's tempting Caramel pudding."

I felt thrilled that my mother praised me in front of him. Perhaps Tanmay had understood what was this all about. I wish he knew why I was nervous and my effort to impress him with the pudding. I wished I could tell him that the lunch tasted so good only because he was sitting next to me. It was the best lunch I had ever had in the entire year. I was looking forward to more happenings in this vacation.

After lunch, we played a game. The first person had to say a word, and then the next person had to say a word he finds in closest association to it. We started...

We always started all games from Pinakin. He was the youngest and the most adorable brother.

He said, "Sweet."

Lalit said, "Tasty."

Ritwik yelled, "Food!"

Parag smiled, "Meena Aunty."

My father said, "Love."

It was my chance, I said, "Tanmay."

I quickly realised what I had blurted out in the chain of words.

I hurriedly corrected my mistake and said, "Tanmay, it's your turn." And began helping my mother clear the plates.

I realised that he had noticed. He knew now I loved him. I had tried giving him a hint. We played many more games, sung songs and then Lalit declared that all of us should play football. He said, and so it was done. Exhausted with prickly heat, we all came home late evening after a day full of fun. However, one thing constantly bothered my mind. The brotherly behaviour of Tanmay did not show the slightest trace of love. My cousins were a few years younger; had Tanmay opened up in front of the younger cousins, they would not have ever understood what was going on between us. They were too young for this. There was no reflection of any memory of what had happened last summer. Tanmay acted so normally that the attention and attraction that I was yearning for was nowhere seen. Perhaps I had to wait for 'that particular time' to look for any further cues.

16

The most unexpected

It was Sunday the other day, so my father was home. Whenever he had leisure time, he joined us. That day he took us out for lunch to a South Indian restaurant. I wore my birthday dress which I had reserved for this day. It was a bright red t-shirt and smart navy-blue bell-bottom faded jeans. I had even made sure I was tuned to the latest fashion like Tanmay. We had a heavy lunch and returned home. After a lazy day, we were looking forward to the terrace time.

The night spread its wings, and the breeze blew away all the traces of boredom, making us as fresh as flowers again. We gathered on the terrace. I was enjoying myself, secretly looking at Tanmay with one eye and the stars in the sky with the other. Tanmay had a great interest in astronomy. He was discussing with my father about a workshop he had attended related to astronomy. Tanmay was good at impressing elders with his 'Mr Know-it-all' image. After a couple of hours, we got ready to bed. But, to my dismay, my mother and father decided to join us on the terrace during the night.

As Tanmay started laying mattresses, I took place in between Parag and Pinakin. Both of them were talking about the *groupism* in their class and how the boys had decided not to speak to girls. They were constantly pulling me into their conversation, but I was too upset to participate. I tried to share some stories in my school, but my ear was tuned to Tanmay's whispers with my father. I was continuously thinking of Tanmay. I found the distance of a few feet like miles. I could not resist this silent distance that separated us now. The night was very long, and I badly longed to speak to Tanmay. My restless, uneasy eyes could not shut. I spent yet another night with disturbed sleep. The next day after feasting on Pav Bhaji, we all dispersed to our rooms to get ready to go out.

I went to my washroom for a bath, leaving the door of the room open. After a hot shower, I came out in a towel, and the very moment Tanmay entered. He closed the door with a wink. I was so anxious that I wanted to rush to the bathroom and hide. But his captivating eyes stopped me. They froze me then and there, making me speechless. I felt as if he was going to express that my ears longed to hear. I felt so nervous and anxious that I wished I could hide myself. In no time, I found Tanmay walking towards me with a manly swag. I was so embarrassed to make eye contact that I kept on looking at the floor. The footsteps grew louder, and I sensed that he was coming near me. My heart thumped harder in excitement, and my body craved desperately for his touch. But at the same time, I felt like running away. Though I did not want it, it was the only thing I wanted at that point in time.

Tanmay got closer to me and pulled my head down with his hands. He lifted my face facing the floor and kissed my lips. I was about to whisper, *'I love you'* so that he will say 'I love you too', but one more time, my words were unheard and unspoken under his overwhelming touch. His touch put a spell, and I became speechless. I felt like the dry arid earth getting drenched in the long-awaited heavy rains. In no time, I was lost in the swirling mist of the first kiss in my life. He undid my towel, and it fell off on the floor. I was lost in him, and he touched me everywhere except my heart.

There was a knock on the door. "Sameer..." called my dad, "I need the iron. It's in your room... can you open the door?" Tanmay rushed inside the bathroom for his bath, leaving me vulnerably alone to face my father. I picked up the towel lying on the floor and wrapped it around my waist. I quickly rushed to unbolt and open the door in a state of panic. I tried to hide my face in the nearest wardrobe to pose that I am searching for my clothes. My father was in an extreme hurry and left the room immediately after taking the iron. I heaved a sigh of relief.

17

My birthday gift

My birthday was on Monday, so my parents joined us on the terrace on Sunday night. I was utterly disappointed. The long night passed, and my cousins woke me up with a huge surprise the next morning. They had decorated the terrace with balloons. They had also planned a small celebration for me in the evening. I had invited my friends to the evening party. My mother had cooked my favourite cuisine, 'Puran Poli' and had ordered a chocolate cake.

My heart was dancing in the seventh heaven. My cute little cousin brothers had made beautiful greetings for me. I felt very special. Everyone gave me gifts, except for Tanmay. I felt sad initially, but I consoled myself thinking, he being there was a huge gift in itself.

The evening celebrations began as soon as my friends came. I felt overjoyed. I was super excited to introduce Tanmay to my friends. But when they met him, he acted very formal and did not mingle with them much. Finding a reason to help my mother, he disappeared into the kitchen. I felt a little hurt by his behaviour. After the celebrations ended and my friends went away, the wave of joy receded, and my negative thoughts took over.

How I wished he could have been a little friendly with them and warmly welcomed them. How I wished he could have confessed his love today. But he was extremely indifferent. Except for a formal handshake and participating in my birthday preparations, he stayed away from me. He did not even hug me once! A hug could have been ordinary and would have easily fit into his brotherly image.

After struggling with my miserable thoughts, I tried to justify him, trying to feel good with whatever he offered. I reassured myself that the terrace time was nearer, and there was still a chance to get a special gift that he might have in his mind.

The weather that evening was relatively pleasant. The cool breeze blew, drying up our sweaty bodies. The sky was cloudy and slowly was getting darker as clouds of rain engulfed the land. It felt so romantic now. But soon, it started thundering, and the rain started pelting down. My mother came upstairs to call us down, yelling, "Kids, don't get wet in the rain... you will catch a cold. Come downstairs."

We all rushed downstairs as Tanmay evacuated the terrace on which my cousins had already started dancing. I wanted to see Tanmay get wet in the rain. But he asked us to go to the kitchen where my mother was making coffee for all of us.

Handing over the tray of cups to Tanmay, she said, "Tanmay, you sleep in Sameer's room, and you three naughty boys, you sleep in the guest room. It's freezing cold right now, and it will be difficult to sleep on the floor." Her words struck me like cupid arrows. I felt so overwhelmed, confused, and awkward. That very moment, I cast a look around and saw Tanmay smiling.

My heart yelled with happiness, 'yippee'. I knew his smile showed an intention. It looked like the excitement in his mind was showing up on his face.

The rainy evening had an induced effect on my heart. I felt an uncontrollable elation, and at the same time, I was nervous and hesitant. I finished my dinner quickly. I felt like running away. I told my mother that I am sleepy and went to my bedroom. Though I wanted that 'special birthday gift', at the same time, I wanted to avoid intimacy. My bedroom had a double bed. Sharing it with Tanmay meant sleeping like a couple. I craved for his love but not intimacy. Though I desired intimacy, I also yearned for a mushy talk.

Turning on my side and facing the wall, I kept a blanket for Tanmay and acted as if I was fast asleep. Tanmay came inside the room. He saw that the lights were switched off and could not see my face. He carefully bolted the door, making no noise, removed his shirt, exposing his hairy chest and silently slid into the bed. I was very scared of his move. I understood he was approaching me. I heard the crunching sound on the plastic bag on which he stepped by mistake. I silently heard him get into the bed. He unfolded his blanket. I tightly closed my eyes and clenched my fists tight. Though I felt an intense attraction for him, I was afraid of him now. I was not prepared for what was going to happen. The dim light of the night lamp could not hide it from Tanmay. Tanmay noticed that I was stressed. He unclenched my fists softly. While he caressed my hair lovingly and pulled me towards him, none of us uttered a word. I wanted to stop him, hold him with my hands and tell him that I wanted to have a deep heart to heart talk. But his behaviour suggested that I was not supposed to say anything. Our movements were silent. His loving hands slowly undressed me. Whatever was happening was very new to me. His experienced hands dominated my fumbling ones. I felt ecstatic. He embraced me and made me his. All was so perfect like I had imagined in my fantasies.

But something unexpected was waiting for me ahead. He turned me on my tummy. I heard him finding something in his bag on the side table. Even in the dark, I saw him open a tube. He forced something inside me. The wetness of the jelly-like substance felt weird. After a moment, I felt him inside, with the sudden unexpected pain. I dare not resist or say a word, but yes, it was not something nice; it was hard-core lust. He tried to penetrate me, giving me intense pain and unimaginable discomfort.

I tried to forcefully push him away, but he got even closer to me and whispered, "Shh, a few more moments, and you will get the pleasure. Try to find pleasure in this pain." But I couldn't; I felt filthy and sticky inside. After one long minute, he ejaculated inside me.

He whispered in my ears, "Happy Birthday," and bit it. He wiped it out with a tissue, and he disposed of his condom in his handbag. He flipped me on my back again and smiled at me. I was so tired and so consumed, the ideas of romance, love had vanished overnight. I loved the foreplay but not sex. Honestly speaking, I hated it. I had seen it in pornographic movies, but seeing and doing something were drastically two different things. I was expecting a beautiful birthday gift but not something as painful as this. He noticed my expressions and softly whispered, "Didn't like it? No problem. Let's not do it again. I dare not say anything, I felt ghastly and repulsed. He took the blanket over his body, trying to sleep and saw me sleeping with back towards him as I curled up like a baby. He said, "Don't worry, sleep will do you good. You will be fine tomorrow morning."

I was naïve and an inexperienced soul. I felt like someone had raped me in and out. The feeling was terribly unpleasant. It felt like someone had tampered with my organs. But I forgave him because I truly loved him. With great difficulty, suppressing the pain in my mind, I tried to search for some happiness in his satisfaction. But it wasn't easy at all.

The whole night I kept thinking. I knew what I had done was wrong. I felt a strong sense of guilt. The physical pain was so excruciating that it even numbed my emotions. I was an innocent boy brought up in a stereotypical Indian ethical and moral background. I did feel at that time, all the values my parents had inculcated in me were at stake. I was no longer someone whom they would feel proud of. I don't remember when I fell asleep. The next morning, I opened my eyes and looked around. The bed was neatly made. There was no trace of Tanmay. For a moment, I wondered whether it was a dream. When I looked at my semi-nude image in the mirror, I noticed some marks of Tanmay's nails on my chest. It reminded me that, yes, the whole thing did happen.

In the morning, I got yet another scary experience. When I passed the bowel, I had unbearable pain. My anal area was bleeding, and I did not know whether to ask Tanmay or my father. But one thing was clear that I could ask none. I was fighting this all alone. I had no courage to step out of the room. I gathered my guts and peeped outside the room. I saw my cousins and Tanmay watching some television show with my mother and father.

The moment I came out, Tanmay shouted, "Hey Sameer, come and join us! You are late!" Tanmay's natural behaviour shocked me. I wondered how he could forget last night. But he acted that way every day. I could not believe how he can be so normal after such incidents when I was shaken in and out. I loathed our relationship at that moment. The nights that I found happy, thrilling, and adventurous now felt like a desert; horrible, emotionless, and full of disillusionment. We never had sex after that one last time. I avoided sleeping beside him on the terrace and never let him a chance to get physical with me. What shocked me even more was my rejection seemed to affect him in no way. Time passed quickly, and it was the time to speak my valedictory words to dear Tanmay. He left for Mumbai, saying nothing but placid and plain 'see you soon'.

18

Battling with the 'other me'

I have always relished watching the sunrise. The day after my cousins left, I woke up early in the morning and went on the terrace to watch the sunrise. Against the erotic nights on the terrace, the bright sun shone. I wanted to reflect on the path I had come a long way in a new light. This was the first time I had fallen in true love. But his lust had destroyed its purity. Our relationship felt murky now. The guilt of getting physically intimate had choked my emotions. I wasn't able to forgive myself. After that one sex, the sweetness I found in our physical love was tarnished. But somewhere, I argued with my own thinking, *'If everything was fair in love, why wasn't I able to forgive myself for what I had done?'* I wanted to forgive him too. While I hated him for some reasons, I was equally worried about losing him. I had avoided physical intimacy with him after that one time, but now I desperately craved for it. I was scared that he would never give me a chance again. But was it worth it? Was it better I had stopped getting intimate? But my love was true, so I had every reason to pursue it. My thoughts ran helter-skelter. I stopped my self-talk for a moment. It was getting so complicated! At a point,

I was unable to think. My head was getting heavier, and I decided to give up all negative thoughts and maintain my trust and belief in my true love and wait.

My life was never going to be a cakewalk, and I had to accept it. I had found someone who liked me, and I loved him. I was brooding over and over, and rather than sorting my thoughts, I was getting more and more muddled up in this marshy mess. So I decided to stop thinking and leave things to destiny.

* * *

Disturbed with contradictory thoughts, I planned a meet-up with my friends that day. We met at our regular hang out spot after a long time. They had returned to Vivek, Akash, and Pranit; we were sitting all in a row on the steps.

Akash stood up and rested his hand on my shoulder. "Tell us what it is. You are no longer the same. I have never seen you so lost and confused. I can't say you are depressed, but at times I really feel something is hurting you deep inside. What's wrong with you, Sameer?"

"Well, I miss him," I said in a low voice.

"Oh common, then why don't you call him up and speak to him?" asked Pranit, smiling.

Now I had no option but to confide in him and speak out the truth. Gathering my guts, I said, "I haven't told you one thing. We are not in a real relationship. We have just got physical. He has never confessed his love, though I have tried many times. Due to lack of love, I loathe our physical intimacy now."

My friends frowned.

"How could you hide this important thing from us?" said Akash, feeling terribly shocked. "Do you even understand what difference it makes?" he literally shouted at me in exasperation.

"Are you mad, Sameer? Can't you understand what this means?" asked Vivek.

"He has never spoken to me like a boyfriend from the day it started. It has been a year now. We used to make out on the terrace when my brothers were fast asleep. We also had sex, but after that, I never let him get physical with me. I thought that must have hurt him, but it did not seem to matter to him at all. Despite getting so many opportunities with me alone, he never said, 'those three words', which I craved for more than anything else in this world. I hated the sex, so we never had it again." I continued with my monologue without reacting to their reactions.

"This is unbelievable!" mumbled Pranit.

"He has loved me in bed but behaved like a brother outside. He has never spoken about his emotions, even after my constant attempts to him do so. On the one hand, I trust and love him, and on the other, I can't tolerate this dual level behaviour anymore. I don't understand how he can move on so easily, as if I don't matter to him. How can he forget me and accept my decision of not getting physical? I can't believe how he can be okay when nothing is okay between us..." saying that, I stopped my breathless monologue.

"Hold on, Sameer, if all that you said now is true, then it raises a serious question mark on your relationship. You better stop that sexual nonsense with him till he says he loves you," said Akash. Akash had an elder sister and learned a lot about the love life from her. How people behave differently with different intentions. She was a love guru in her college. So, Akash knew it all.

There was a long pause that followed Akash's words, and it turned my world upside down. It was evident that everyone agreed with him. I was about to narrate my first sexual experience, which was really painful, but the kind of cross-questioning that was going to come up from them pulled me back. I had to break the ice somehow. Trying to take the conversation in a positive direction, I said, "I agree."

"But we also share a wonderful bond. In spite of all this, we have great understanding. Maybe the family and social pressures pull him behind." I tried to give a lame justification for his behaviour. I did not like others being judgemental about him.

"Family and social pressures, that's okay. But it is you who is assuming things. This love is your imagination. I find this guy of yours very weird. From what you have narrated, it clearly indicates he is playing with your needs," said Pranit.

"Even I am utterly shocked that he never said anything verbally. You have been alone together so many times, and there should be no reason why he did not get a chance to express his emotions. Try to understand, there are people who become intimate to fulfill their bodily needs. You need not assume it is love," said Vivek.

"I think you are living in a fool's paradise. There cannot be any other reason behind this double standard behaviour," added Akash.

"See, Sameer, if you had got opportunities to speak when you were alone, where did those pressures of society come into the picture? Please don't justify his behaviour. I am being upfront and blunt... he is exploiting you. Forget about love... you are just his use and throw thing after a blow-off."

I felt as if I had lost some race. I reluctantly agreed. I knew there was no point in defending his side when I sought their advice. They were my friends and my well-wishers too. I said, "You are right. I will try to find out the truth. But he has been very caring and protective as a brother. Isn't that a sign of love? He might get offended if I ask. What if you guys are being paranoid, and he is simply poor at expression? I think I will wait, not let my emotions flow and see what happens next."

I quickly changed the topic by turning to Vivek. "So, how is your college life? Did you like any hot boy in your tuition classes?" We started gossiping again. I heard new stories about another gay couple whom Akash knew. While the bla-bla-bla went on, I felt terribly upset. Somewhere I began doubting the trueness of our relationship. I was with them physically, but my heart and soul weren't. But today, nothing filled me with vigour like it usually did. I felt like I am a big loser but did not want to reveal it to them. After some time, I returned home, carrying huge, burdensome baggage full of thoughts and doubts which I was planning to dispose of permanently. I, one more time, tried to trust my honest love, and I knew one thing whether he loved me or not, my love had the power to make him love me.

19

A different me

I engaged myself in my routine and kept myself busy to help overcome my emotions. I was done with my ninth standard, and I had my future ahead. I had to perform well in the most important academic year waiting. It was the deciding year of my career. I had to cross this major milestone in my school life with flying colours to move to the next level. So, I decided and determined to keep this love story on the back burner till I was done with my board exams.

So now, the nerd was back. I cocooned myself and started studying night and day. At times I fell asleep with a book on my chest. It was then my mother pulled a blanket over me, switched off the lights and went away. In the recent test, my scores were unexpectedly poor despite this tremendous effort. My parents thought it was because I had not joined any tuition class.

One day, after I returned from school, I was sitting with my mother and father having snacks.

"Sameer, you seem to be overburdened with studies. I have hardly seen you smiling these days. Let's go for a movie if you need change." My dad tried to be very supportive, like always.

"No, Dad, I am not in that mood. I hope the year rolls away quickly." I knew what had taken away my smile.

"Are you stressed, my son?" dad asked me, cleaning his spectacles with his t-shirt. He appeared very loving when he looked at me this way.

"Well, yes, all my friends have tuition classes, and I did not join any because I thought that it would be a waste of time," I said.

"That is what we had been telling you since last year that you better join some private coaching class. But you were always reluctant and said that self-study suits you better and you don't need one," interrupted my mother.

"Yes, Mom, but the conditions have changed now. I did not know mathematics this year is not so easy."

"I badly need a coaching class for maths if I have to give my best shot during the exams. But those classes are so packed with students that one cannot get any personal attention. A lot of time gets wasted in commuting as well. I think I need a personal tutor to save time. Do you know anyone who can visit our home and teach me?" I asked them.

My mother said, "Oh yes! I think I know someone who might be interested. Suchitra's daughter has come back to Pune. I remember my friend saying a few years back that she was extremely good at maths. She also loves teaching. I will ask Suchitra if she is interested. She must be a few years senior to you. She was in your school, I remember. She has been a meritorious student throughout her academic career."

"Alright, mom, that will be an excellent idea. As she stays nearby, it will save my travelling time too. Please ask her and tell me what she says."

I wanted to give a fresh start to my life. There was one more reason why I wanted to avoid coaching classes. They were a hub for girls and boys to interact with one another and a place where we could see love stories flowering and weaning. I wanted to keep myself away from the world of love and attraction. So the only option was to avoid such exposure. I wished I could put my head in the books and never get distracted by such a thing again. If my love for Tanmay was true, he would come back to me one day and the way I wanted. It would be him who would contact me again and not me calling him with stupid excuses to speak. I had decided to wait and watch. It was easier said than done. I battled mood swings every day, and the tears in my eyes did not allow me to sleep at night. My tears kept on smudging the ink of my textbooks.

20

A new buddy

So Preeti said yes... and I found a friend and a tutor in her. Preeti was an IT engineer, and she was here in Pune for an assignment. She worked in an IT company in the US. I always felt fortunate to have found her. She was an average looking girl, but with the most beautiful smile I had ever seen. With her simple clothes and a smile full of kindness, she looked so adorable. She was an extremely understanding, mature, young girl of twenty-two. She was disciplined, punctual, and highly particular.

Though I learnt maths from her, she gave me a treasure of life lessons. As days passed, I started finding a friend in her. I started sharing every little thing that happened in my school. I visited her home every Saturday and Sunday when she was free from work, and she taught me for around three hours. After we finished our class, she offered me a cup of coffee, and we chitchatted on the terrace balcony of her flat.

On one such winter Sunday, she started telling me about an episode of ragging with a friend of hers. Something in me opened an old chamber of pain and insecurities in the past. I said, "Preeti, even I had been a victim of ragging. The boys in our class mocked me because they found my expressions and my mannerisms effeminate. They criticized my interests and made fun of me because I enjoyed playing female roles in skits."

She said, "It doesn't matter how you look. If you ask me from the point of view of girls, you will look like a chocolate hero when you grow up. Wait, let me show you something."

She went into her room and brought a photo, an old photo of a girl and a boy in school uniform. "Don't you think this boy looks like you?" she asked.

"Umm, yes, a bit," I replied.

"The girl is you and the boy?"

"This is Rohan and me. He is my childhood friend and now my fiancée. Look at him now," saying she showed me another photo.

"Doesn't he look manly now?"

"He is handsome."

"So, don't think about how you look. You look good, and you will look very handsome when you grow up. Don't think about what your classmates say. Looks don't matter. What matters is how good your heart is."

Looks did not matter, even I knew that. Even I knew I was handsome. But I was gay. I wished I could confide the bitter truth with her someday. Well, Suchitra aunty being my mother's friend, I dare not tell her that.

"Always remember, only weak people mock others. Strong people forget it and ignore such attempts. So learn to forgive others for their mistakes. It relieves most of the burden, anger and negative emotions in your mind," she said. But these words were undoubtedly enlightening and motivating. I loved discussing philosophical stuff with her.

Learning maths from her proved to be my best decision ever. She managed to finish my syllabus in five months. But then it was her time to go back to the US. Her six-month assignment was over. She was going to get engaged with Rohan. I was very happy for her. But the parting grief rested heavily on my mind. My gay friends were busy with their college life. I had isolated myself from them this year to achieve what I wanted. I missed them, and now I was going to miss her too. I was already missing Tanmay. Missing was so painful, I thought. I wished she should have married and settled down in Pune. At least, I would not have lost a new friend I had found. But this is how life was. You find someone special, and moments with that person become worth treasuring; it's very time you lose them. This had happened with my gang, my dear Tanmay, and now it was Preeti.

21

Moving on

Time flies faster when we get busier, and that is exactly what happened this year. Staying away from friends, family friends, and, more importantly, my gay gang and Tanmay's thoughts was the most difficult thing to do. But the best part was I did accomplish it. Time flew before I could realise, and the exams came to an end. I started waiting for summers with the hope to be successful in my love life this time. However, my parents planned a trip to Kerala to celebrate my vacations, so we had to cancel the plan to invite our cousins to our place. I felt very sad, how I wish I could tell them to cancel the trip to Kerala. But I dare not tell them this.

One day my father asked me, "Sameer, you have been bugging for the last two years that you wanted to go to Kerala. Now when we are going, why do you look so disappointed?"

"Nothing, dad. I am just tensed about the results." My dad had planned a great trip, especially for me, so I had to lie. The grief of not meeting Tanmay was trickling down inside me. I had to wrap up my emotions and lock them in the closet of my heart helplessly. Though

I tried doing so, during the entire tour, I kept on missing him. While travelling by car from one city to another, I imagined Tanmay sitting beside me and me resting my head on his shoulder. While sailing through the Allepey backwaters, how I wished it could have been us. When I saw couples taking poses in the lush green tea gardens of Munnar, I missed him even more. How romantic it would have been to get cosy together in this pleasant weather, I thought. I felt so incomplete without him. After bathing in the beauty of nature in Kerala, we came back from the vacation.

My parents were eagerly waiting for my result the next day. Everyone thought I would be the topper in my class, and my name would flash in the merit list. But it was not the case, I ranked sixth in my school, and I had scored 90%. I knew well that I would have been the topper had he not been there in my life. Though my parents were not happy, they weren't worried much. My score was good enough to get enrolled into a decent college.

My dad said, "Sameer, you lost your rank because of your stress and nothing else."

"It's okay, Sushant. Let him not think about it. The rat race would always trouble him later. There are bigger things in life he has to achieve," my mother tried to console me indirectly.

I felt low; my effort was in vain. I knew well I was the one who was responsible for it. I decided to meet my gang to lift my mood. Though we had parted ways, we made it a point to meet up when any one of us needed support during the bad times.

My friends understood well what had affected my scores. I felt better after meeting them. I was thrilled to reunite with them. They were already into the college, and soon our topics were going to be common. Now it was the time to enjoy life and have fun. However, one thing came upon me as a shock. Tanmay did not call me to ask about my results. I felt rejected and ignored. I had almost decided to give up my hope to seek his love.

I started meeting my gay friends every day. Every evening was full of hot gossips, dirty talks, deep sharing and whatnot. My life was getting more difficult, and somewhere I felt that I needed to detach myself from Tanmay if I wanted to live a stable life. I did not share Tanmay's behaviour with my friends, for I knew that they will end up saying he played with my life. Whether he loved me or not, I could never withstand any criticism about him. I tried to digest my emotions on my own, stamped them underneath my feet and moved ahead in my life. I found it so difficult, but that was the only solution left. I had a hope that somewhere in a small corner of my heart that one day I would hear those magical words from him.

22

Time flies

I stepped into the college. I felt like a free bird. Being in love with Tanmay, no boy in college caught my eyes. Hiding my gay identity and putting on a mask of a nerd helped me escape ragging, survive, and thrive in college. One of the interesting things in my life was many of the pretty faces in college had a thing for me. I often heard girls calling me 'cutie'. Most of the girls liked my company and respected me. Maybe because I gave more importance to their hearts and brains, unlike others or perhaps because they found me more understanding.

One day after the physics lecture, my friend Nisha came running after me. She was the sweetest girl in our class. This bubbly girl with a cute innocent face and twinkling eyes tied her long hair in a top knot. She usually dressed in bright coloured tops that went with the trendy trousers. Her super maintained figure was still conspicuous from her decent dress and caught the eyes of all boys. She was a good friend of mine, and many believed she had a crush on me.

Nisha kept running behind me, calling me loud in her high pitched voice, "Hey Sam, wait." I stopped. "Tell me, Nisha, what is it that you came running behind me? Any problem?"

"Can you meet me today in the evening? I have something important to tell you."

"Alright, then meet me at the canteen before you go home," I said.

"No, Sam, can we meet at Starbucks?"

"Oh no, it's very expensive, let's meet in the canteen. What's wrong with the place?"

Reluctantly, she agreed. We met in the canteen, and she said she would speak to me on the phone as she wasn't comfortable. I asked her what it was, but she was reluctant to share. She just gave me a big envelope and said I should open it when I go home.

When I went home, I checked my mobile. It was a big shock! I had received a picture message saying *'I love you'* with loads of many more text messages about her feelings for me. When I checked the envelope, I found a beautiful greeting saying, *'I love you'*. I knew how rejections felt in life, but I had no option but to confide the truth. I thought a lot about how to react, and I called her after half an hour.

"Hi, Nisha! I just checked your messages."

"So...?" she asked coyly, almost panting. The girl otherwise bold was shy today, and I could hear her breath.

"Nisha, I can completely understand your feelings, but I have no such feelings for you because I am gay. But I beg of you, please don't reveal this to anyone."

"What!? I can't believe this." Her reaction came out with a blast.

"Yes, my dear friend. You will always be sisterly to me. I already have someone in my life. See, Nisha, you are attractive, intelligent, and sweet. Anyone whom you like can fall for you."

"But why did you flirt with me?" she said angrily, sobbing at the same time.

"I never flirted with you... I was just being nice to you," I tried to explain calmly.

"But how is that possible? You don't look gay," she asked me angrily.

"Nisha, I have a body of a man, but my gender, that is, my feelings, are different. I like men. You can say I am a cis man. I purposely make sure that my mannerisms look like a man so that my gender wasn't conspicuous from my behaviour. I have been a victim of ragging before and wanted to make sure I won't be one now. So, to show others, I behave like other men."

"Sameer, I feel you are lying. Please tell me frankly if you like some girl and you are making up this story to get rid of me. Please don't play 'hide and seek' with my emotions. Tell me the truth once, and I will move on. You don't have to tell me you are gay to push me away."

"I am not pushing you away. I like you as a friend and as a person. And yes, I do have someone in my life, and he is a man. So please believe my words."

"Oh, so you are really gay," and she started weeping again.

"Yes, Nisha. I wish I were not, but this is the dark truth."

"Sameer, I loved you so much," her words were muffled in tears. But why did you keep on making passes on me? Was it to show other boys that you are just like them?" asked Nisha feeling unsure about my intentions.

"No, my dear, I genuinely felt you deserved all those compliments. I still feel you are very gorgeous. I wasn't doing this as a part of any plan."

"Sameer, you have no idea how deeply I am involved in you. Next time you speak to girls, make sure you keep your distance. But please do a favour, don't talk to me or I will love you more. I don't think I will be able to be friends with you anymore. I will speak to you in the college tomorrow. I am not in a condition to talk now. Sorry Sameer," she said, almost crying like a child.

"Nisha... listen..." *beep*

She disconnected the call. I let her have her own space and did not call her back. She was heartbroken. I felt sad for her. I could sense what she must have felt. At least it would be easy for her to accept it and move once she learnt that I am gay. But it became more difficult for her to be friends with me. She kept on avoiding confrontations with me, and it felt like I lost a true friend. I only hoped she would not disclose my orientation to anyone, and yes, she did not.

Two more girls asked me out after this incident. What I wanted from Tanmay, I got it from girls. I had learnt that my life would be this way; I had to accept it and move on with time. The better side of my college life was, unlike my school days, I had a pretty good, decent friends circle. None of them suspected I was gay as I tried not to act like one. When they asked me about my crushes or girls, I did tell them I had a few and said that I was simply shy with girls.

So this was how I mingled with other boys being like one of them. I had become more easy-going and amiable now. My college kept me happy during the day, but when I came back, the memories with Tanmay in every nook and corner of the house reminded me of him at night. Whenever I saw girls and boys dating in the college canteen, I always wished I could date him. Though not now, I always hoped that someday, Tanmay and I would become a couple and date the way others do. Fighting with the pendulum of my thoughts and emotions had become a way of life.

* * *

One day, my mom rushed into my room, bubbling with excitement. "Sameer, Tanmay has got enrolled in a very reputed university in Germany for MBA. Do call him and congratulate him!" I was overjoyed for my dear Tanmay. I had a reason to call him now, and I had to call him to celebrate his happiness though he never called me on his own. I had accepted the fact that this would probably reduce the frequency of our meetings. With no commitment and emotional involvement, it was impossible to understand where our relationship was heading. But this time, I was going to act more maturely. I was not going to be clingy even on a call with him. With this uncertainty and insecurity, in the torment of one-sided longing, my emotions had dried up a bit

With great self-control and gathering strength, I called him. We spoke to each other heartily, and I conveyed to him my best wishes. He gave me best wishes for my college life but very formally. Since he did not speak about our relationship, I decided to continue with my reserved attitude.

I accepted that I had to wait till we meet to find answers to all questions in my mind. I finally determined and tried to divert my attention to friends and family.

For almost six months, I faced terrible emotional ups and downs. Slowly and steadily, I was getting over my past. I was achieving the impossible. I knew that my love for Tanmay will have to wait for the right time to come. So, I learnt to live my life with no expectations. But destiny never loved my peace.

23

College days

One day I returned from my college and rang the doorbell. I waited for my mother to open the door. But my mother did not come, and the door was opened. I could not believe my eyes. It was Tanmay in front of me in flesh and blood. The moment my eyes met his, my dried emotions melted away. It seemed that the river of my emotions across which I had built a huge dam had crashed with the intensity built up in my heart. My heart was brimmed with those memories. I kept looking into his eyes, searching to find his unspoken words. Looking at my lost look, he brought me back to reality, saying, "How was the surprise?" His voice quenched my thirsty heart, and I blushed. So, my true feelings had some hopes of reciprocation. My self-control vanished in no time, and I fell for his charm again.

As I stepped inside the house, my mother said, "Tanmay surprised all of us! He came back from Germany last week and wants to meet all his relatives before he goes back again."

My thoughts were muddled up, and I was thoughtless as usual. I secretly checked my reflection in the cabinet glass of the kitchen to check whether I looked presentable or not. I was tanned and wondered if he would like me more this way or he would like me more if I looked fairer. I noted that he would surely notice that I had grown up. I had a light moustache now and though uneven, some traces of stubbles. How I regretted postponing my shaving plan to tomorrow. I had grown taller and looked more attractive. I wondered if Tanmay had noticed the changes in me.

"Dude, go to your room, change and come back. Till then, I will chitchat with aunty. I have so many things to tell you. Be quick."

"Yup, I will just be there," I replied, suppressing my excitement under the glow of my cheeks.

I went to my room to freshen up and was shocked to find Tanmay's stroller there. I had assumed that he would be there only for a couple of hours as his paternal uncle stayed in Pune. But it wasn't so. I knew why he wanted me to go to my room immediately. He wanted me to know that he is going to stay with me. This was an indication of what was waiting for me at night.

I felt the inner heat engulfing my forehead and ears, just with the thought of getting intimate with him. I was happy that though I had avoided physical intimacy last time, he had let me take my time. I was so glad that he was not cross with my rejection. My emotional inhibitions and moral dilemma melted away, unleashing my desire. I quickly changed into the best possible clothes and went to the kitchen. I whispered to my mother, "Mom, is Tanmay staying in my room? Didn't you ask him to go to the guest room?"

"Sameer, it was he who insisted. He said that it would be better to share a room with you than staying alone in the guest room. Aren't you comfortable with his company?"

"Oh, nothing like that, Mom, just asked you casually. At times I study at night, so I thought it would disturb his sleep. I can shift to the guest room if I want to study. Let him stay in my room. It's okay."

"Sameer, you are focussed enough, take a break from your studies this weekend, or else your scores will suffer just like last year. You need to destress yourself. Enough of your sincerity! You are in college now... don't forget to enjoy while you try to get good scores," said my mom lovingly.

I smiled back warmly. My heart took a flight. It was very clear from this incident that he chose to stay with me. This meant that his feelings for me existed in spite of my avoidance. With a gush of excitement, I rushed out and sat on the couch, opposite his chair, with a mug of coffee for us. I had taken enough space to prepare myself to speak to him. I said, "Tanmay, so how many days are you planning to stay here?"

"If you are free, maybe for a couple of days, I was planning to hang out with you in Pune and see places if you have time."

I had got my first confirmation for which I was waiting for. This meant he had been purposely waiting for me to finish with my school and now showed intentions to start with a real relationship.

I could see some progress, so I discarded the plan of questioning him and decided to go with the flow. I was confident about one thing that true love never fails. I was going to make the best of my opportunity now.

This time he behaved as if he was more than a brother and more than a friend. So finally, it was the start of our relationship. We visited malls and tourist spots. I remember even today the way he had pulled me closer on Sinhagad fort for a selfie and kissed me when no one was around. His hand had reached the chain of my jeans, but he withdrew after we heard some whispers of tourists around. It was also the first time that just two of us had lunch and dinners outside. They did not seem like real dates, but somewhere I wished this could mark the beginning. We had a great time together. The days went like this, but the nights got wilder. Though he abstained from sex for me, oral sex was always an option for me to satisfy him. Though I had experienced repulsion last time, his understanding nature encouraged me to please him more. This was the time when I let go of my guilt, my hesitation, my dilemma, and my morals, tarnishing the purity of my love.

This visit of his had given me a feeling that perhaps things would materialize as I grow up. I was getting his quality time, and it was satisfactorily enough. I did not want to confess to him and spoil the flow of the whole affair. I knew it was going to happen one day, for I trusted the strength of my love for him.

After that one visit, he kept visiting me every time he returned from Germany. But the time spent together made me miss him, even more when he was away. But I was convinced by now that Tanmay was poor at expressing his feelings. I found his frequent visits proof of his love. Life had taken a new turn, and there were chances of taking our relationship to the next level. I was going to get a new phone once I get enrolled in an engineering college, which would open doors to our communication. However, I decided that I would take it slow and behave more like a friend than lovers. So, that one or the other day, it might push him to take the initiative.

Our relationship had taken a new leaf, and I was invigorated to nourish our relationship so that one day it would take the shape of the love I was yearning for.

24
A sweet shock

I met Sameer five years back. An obedient and intelligent boy, who was seven years younger than me, became a little friend of mine. In the beginning, the age difference between us seemed to be large, but as Sameer grew older, it almost vanished. His father gifted him a smartphone when he got enrolled in a reputed engineering college in Pune. It was then we reconnected.

I felt so delighted to get in touch with this young friend of mine. After a couple of years, WhatsApp became more common in India, and we became friends in true sense. He must be around twenty at that time.

I remember he always had a keen interest in my work for the LGBTQ community. He followed every post of mine related to it. All the time, he was the first to leave a comment or hit a like on my post. After noticing his deep interest in the life of LGBTQs, one day, I asked him if he would be interested in joining my online campaign and promote it among his relatives and friends.

I was surprised when he hesitated. He repeatedly kept on saying, "Please don't tell your mother or my parents that I am in for your campaign. I will secretly promote it." I was shocked to hear this. I knew his parents were pretty open-minded. I wondered what was pulling him behind. So I probed, "Why are you saying that, Sameer? Even your mother congratulated me with a message when she saw a photo of mine in an 'LGBTQ awareness' rally that I posted on Facebook."

He said nothing, but I could not miss the emotional intensity hiding behind his pause. His constant requests of 'don't tell my mother and father' raised hundreds of questions in my mind. The truth flashed in front of my eyes suddenly, and I guessed it.

"Sameer, can you tell me why are you hesitating? You can share your worries with me. Are you afraid of anything?" I asked.

"Preeti, well, I will tell you but promise me you will keep it a secret," he literally begged.

"God promise," I said.

"I am gay, Preeti."

So my guess had been right.

"Umm... Yes, Preeti. But please don't tell anyone. I have always been hiding my identity. Please, Preeti, being an activist, you are aware of our problems, so please keep it a secret."

"Sameer, don't panic. I will keep it a secret," I assured him.

From that day, we got even closer. He started sharing more about his life, and I could understand him better. Even I had a few friends and colleagues in the US who were gays and lesbians, so I empathized with his every little smile and tear. From that day, I started sharing with him LGBTQ stories of exploitation, success, and pain. This opened his inner compartments, and he began telling him every silly little secret in his life. It could be about Tanmay, his friend Nisha and many other girls who liked him, his gay friends, his petty fights, and arguments with parents and whatnot. He even told me about his romantic nights with Tanmay. He texted me about his JEE class, gossips, college life and the challenges he faced every day while hiding his orientation. As I got closer to Sameer, I started engaging with his parents on video calls and chats. I got closer to them too. His mother always said I had some bonds with their family from the last birth. His bond with me made them feel very carefree about him. I was happy with the bond I shared with him and his family.

The roots of this bond were deep in his teenage. When Sameer was in his tenth, I had just started with my first job. I was 22 then and was going to get married the following year. My fiancée had been my college friend and a family friend too. So, our marriage was the happiest thing to happen to us as well as our families. We were on the verge of a relationship when Rohan was licking his wounds of a break-up. When our parents noticed that our friendship was likely to move one step ahead, they hitched us together forever.

The first three years of our marriage were smooth and happy. Everything was perfect. There was a great understanding between us. As Rohan and I had been friends from childhood, I knew everything about him, in and out. However, the twist in the tale came much later. We had a happy married life for three good years. All was perfect when Rohan had to move to another state for his work. I had never imagined that he could meet someone with whom he fell in love.

I had not thought about this situation even in one of my worst nightmares. One day Rohan called me and said, “I am in love with someone, and I can’t live without her." This one sentence broke everything that was there in between us, and I was badly shattered. With great maturity, we resolved the major issues in our marriage, and the divorce followed. The divorce brought me depression, pain, dejection, and frustration. To get it over with, I got more involved in social activities. That was the time when I actively started working as an LGBTQ activist. I found a channel to divert my energy.

Around the same time, I reconnected with Sameer. The roots of the old bond gave green shoots to our relation. The understanding man in Sameer had begun to sprout, and the vulnerable woman in me needed his supporting shoulder. We complemented each other well. His compassionate, empathetic nature eased my grief bringing us even closer.

I always felt I would have loved to have someone like him in my life after Rohan and I separated. I adored Sameer a lot. He was good looking, intelligent, and a very decent person. He was gay, so neither did I let my feelings bud nor let them blossom.

After he confided that he was gay and opened up more on such topics, he told me his biggest secret. He told me about his and Tanmay's relationship. He narrated how they started dating and how things were slowly changing. I always felt happy that he had someone in his life. There were so many gays I had heard who tried to get involved in flings only because they had no genuine relationship. There were so many who stayed single because they did not find a good match. I thought, '*What if it was his brother? The good part was he wasn't alone.*' I always asked him more, but he told me nothing except how he touched him for the first time, and the same thing happened over and over. When I asked him, "When did he propose you or asked you out?" He changed the topic. I wondered why. He never talked more about it. However, as years passed, Sameer kept telling me that their relationship was slowly progressing, and one day, he was going to propose to Tanmay if it did not come from him.

As time passed, our bond ripened. He now knew everything about my life, and I loved the way he understood my emotions. It could be the most trivial in our life; we always shared it with each other. He had also helped me a lot to get over my divorce and find happiness in a single life. We had started becoming the best buddies.

It could be any hour of the night or any minute of our busy days, we were always available for each other. May it be his exams or some important deadline at my office, we always managed to find the time.

I always felt that maybe he was not single, and I was, so he did not express things to me about their relationship. I kept a distance when he was reluctant to reveal those things. He never disclosed details about their chats, calls and love talks in general. Maybe he avoided it as it would remind me of my relationship with Rohan, I thought.

Whenever I felt low and insecure, he made all possible efforts to lift my mood up. He cracked jokes with his silly sense of humour, making me smile. It was not with his sense of humour but with his cute efforts. Though I was elder to him, sometimes I felt that he could understand me more than anyone else in this world. No matter what our ages, genders, or sexual orientations were, it was just impossible to find a better friend. I liked him, as a person and as a man too. But he was gay, and it wasn't a good idea to fall in love with him. So I restricted my emotions and was happy with the bond we shared, cherished, and carefully nourished in the best possible way.

26

History repeats

My college life was very fast-paced. While juggling with studies, fun, JEE classes, and my emotional ups and downs, life had become a roller coaster. With the hope of a happy future with Tanmay, I focussed on my own life, determined to not repeat the mistake I made during my SSC exams. I was not going to let this relationship hamper my scores one more time. I studied smartly this time, and I did fairly well and landed safely in a good engineering college. College days were going smooth till date until one day.

It was Pari who came to me like a saviour that day. I still remember my state of panic when I had lost my journal two hours before my viva. If I had not found my file, I would have ended up with a 'backlog' for the next semester. I had searched my file everywhere but could not find it. I had totally given up hopes. Tears were waiting in my eyes, but they dare not come out in the crowded classroom. After few minutes, there was a tap on my shoulder. I turned behind to see a heavily made-up Pari. She handed over the file to me and gave me a sensuous smile. I awkwardly smiled back in return and extended my hand to take it.

"No, not till you promise me that you will come out with me for dinner," she said, teasing me.

I was so stressed and needed the file urgently. I had to do a quick revision and had no time to think, so hurriedly, I said, "Of course! Why not? Thank you so much, Pari."

She handed over the file to me and went away playing with her curly hair, which let loose balancing herself on her high heels. Though a shady character, she was my saviour, so I tried to be as nice as possible. I felt no harm in going out with her on the offer of getting my lost file back. I buried my head in the file and revised all I had studied.

After I finished my viva, I was on my way back home when she blocked my way at the gate of my college campus.

"Hey, boy stop, where are you going? You look very sexy in these formals that you are wearing today," she said with a naughty smile.

I tried giving a forced smile. Her words made me uncomfortable, and I felt very embarrassed. She was quite loud, and it scared me even more because a college campus was certainly not the place for such conversations.

"How was your viva? I am going home," I tried to change the topic.

"Hey, why not plan a stay somewhere this weekend?" and she winked.

I was shocked by this offer. I did not know what to say. I wished I could run away from that place right away. I wondered what if students walking past us must have heard this. Being gay, I was cautious when it came to my image. I took special care that nobody pointed fingers at my character. I was in a fix and could not think of a way out. During such stressful times, I often made blunders and spoke out the truth when not required.

I said, "Sister, I am gay. You have taken me wrong."

"Doesn't matter, try me, and you will develop a taste for girls!" she said, giving another seductive smile.

That made me even more restless. I felt that people around were staring at us. I wondered what would they think of me if they see her in conversation with me, making such gestures. After all, a man is known by the company he keeps, I thought.

I wished I could hide my face and run away. My hands were sweaty with fear, and my wet feet could feel the dirt that now had got wet with the sweat. I abruptly said, "No thanks Pari, Bye. I am getting late."

She kept calling me, "Hey boy, wait..." I paid no heed to her and rushed home.

* * *

My exams got over, and so did the vacation. The next semester started, and it was the first day of my college. I was greeted with a horrible day. During the first half of the day, like always, my sack was lying on the floor. After some time, when I checked again, it vanished. I knew this was some kind of prank. When I saw it after another fifteen minutes, it was back in place.

During the lunch break, I opened my sack to take out my lunch box. To my shock, numerous loose condoms fell on the floor from it. Some colourful vulgar pictures of straight and gay couples making love tucked in my sack fell on my desk. I put inside everything, quickly closed the chain of my sack, and started running away.

I might have covered ten steps on my way. The moment I found all my classmates staring at my lower body, I stopped. I got confused when all of them started looking at my lower body. I felt awkward and upset. Their behaviour was shocking. I panicked when Ninaad rushed towards me and tore out the paper stuck on my back, saying, *'I am gay! Fuck me at ₹5 per hour'*. I felt my head spinning, and I would faint. The school memories of ragging flashed in front of my eyes, and I freaked out. Ninaad, a good friend of mine, understood my situation and quickly took me away from the scene.

He took me to a nearby eatery on his bike. He placed an order and offered me a glass of water, making me feel comfortable.

"What was that, Sameer?"

"Ninaad that bitch Pari, she asked me out and that too for a one night stand. I denied, so she and her friends framed me into this," I told him, hiding my identity.

"Please complain about this incident," said Ninaad.

"Let us see. I don't want to go against their gang. They might trouble me more."

"But nowadays, the anti-ragging laws are strict, and in our college, it will be taken care of," said Ninaad, trying his level best to convince and protect me.

"Alright, I might. Let's quickly finish and go back and face them. I don't want to show them I got scared or something. I will keep ignoring."

After that incident, many of my well-wishers asked me if I was gay. But I kept telling them I wasn't. When they were still not convinced, I told them how rejecting Pari's offer had trapped me, and Pari and her friends framed me into this. Somehow, I managed to get through the whole prank, but I developed enmity with Pari's group. They kept on spreading gossips about me. I started avoiding interacting with people to run away from it. I did share formal friendly relations with some of my classmates, but all the relations stayed at a distance, on a very superficial level. I was friends with some girls, but unlike my previous full of fun college life, my engineering college had turned me into someone different.

27

The silver linings

In my dry college life, the only interesting part was Tanmay's half-yearly visit. We began to exchange memes and were connected in a friendly, casual way. I made sure not to use any emoticons of love just to make things happen at the right time. We even shared videos of gay lovemaking and dirty jokes. Despite the good bond we shared, we rarely spoke on video calls and only had long chats. I called Tanmay occasionally, and even he did to give best wishes on festivals and my exams. So, the whole communication pattern was exactly like the way it would be in between two straight boys. But I always hoped that the picture would soon change as I felt the bond between us getting better as the days passed. After seeing more of life and feeling more mature, I had learnt to keep my emotions about Tanmay at bay and made an effort to love myself more.

More importantly, I was also getting closer to Preeti, even more than I was to Tanmay. Amidst the uncertainty of my future with Tanmay, my calls and chats with Preeti gave me a life every day. She was the one who helped me face the terrifying times in my college life with great courage. In fact, she gave me the necessary strength to face it, ignore it and move ahead in life.

With her motivation and inspiration, I could spend all these years on my growth. I lived for myself, tried to be in the good books of professors, utilized mass-bunks for personal growth and nothing much. It did not take much time for me to turn twenty-one. I graduated with a distinction and got placed in a reputed multinational company as I had planned earlier. The culture in MNCs had always been supportive to LGBTQs, so there were fewer chances of ragging, and like always, as I remained in the closet, nothing really mattered to me. I had made my parents very happy and proud until now. Life was not going to be that easy later, but meeting their expectations later was going to bring me in a fix.

28

Hopping hurdles

I had recently got promoted with a fat hike after working hard for three years in this company. My parents were pleased to know this. I thought that they were happy as I had met every little expectation they had from me.

But, one morning, I realised I was wrong.

I was woken up with my mom and dad quarrelling and yelling at the top of their voices.

"This is too much. I am not going to wait until his 30s," shouted my angry mother.

"Come on, Mina, why so much haste?" my father sounded irritated.

"My friends keep asking me about Sameer. At Meenakshi's daughter's wedding last month. Mr Sathe seemed very interested in Sameer for his daughter. I want him to start seeing girls now. It's time to get serious about his life now," my mother tried convincing him.

"He is serious enough about life. I don't want him to be more," said my father arrogantly.

"Why don't you understand? If he starts thinking about it now, we can proceed with the whole matter comfortably. He can even date a few girls and decide.

If he has a good friend, we can consider that too." my mother continued feeling exasperated.

"Enough, stop it now! This is not the right time, Mina," said my father.

"But the whole point is, what is wrong in discussing this? If I know his expectations, I can search accordingly. Let us register him on a matrimony site, at least. He will turn twenty-five in the next one month." my mother went on without listening to him.

My father exploded, "In which century are you living in? Nowadays, even girls don't marry at this age. Let him enjoy his life. Why are you in such a great hurry to get him a bride? He is still so young. Have you even seen him around girls? Maybe he is more focused on his profession. Let him enjoy his life and explore relationships. Why are you in such a hurry? I think you should wait till twenty-eight."

"Look, Sushant, last week, I consulted an astrologer for our family. I showed Sameer's horoscope to him. Do you know what he said? If Sameer doesn't marry before 28, he will remain single forever," my mother kept pressing her point, trying her level best to convince him.

"Oh, come on, Mina. You always fall victim to such things. I don't believe a word of that con man of yours. Why couldn't he predict that his own wife would run away with a man after marriage?" my father's words shot like bullets.

Hearing this, I felt my energy draining. This was just a trailer of my future. The day of confrontation was not far anymore.

They heard me in the kitchen, and my mom came out. She served me poha and opened up the topic that was simmering insider her. "Son, you are almost twenty-five.

See, things like marriage take time. I would be very happy if you settle down by twenty-eight. I think you start looking around for nice girls. I have Whatsapped you profile links of some girls. Check them out and let me know if you like anyone." she tried to convince me in the softest possible way.

I was shocked by her planning. "Mother, are you out of your mind? Are you my boss giving me goals and targets with timelines?"

My dad and I both burst out laughing.

He said chuckling, "Your mom is crazy. Man, you enjoy your free life."

"No, son, don't take me wrong, but I don't want you to go with the typical arrange marriage system. The divorce cases are increasing, and I have heard many tragedies from my friends. Don't you have a single friend whom I can consider as a prospective bride? Feel happy I am asking you to find your life partner yourself! My friends are more interested in getting a daughter-in-law of their choice rather than encouraging their sons to choose on their own. Had you told me that you like someone, I wouldn't have bugged you at all. Don't be a workaholic like your dad, Sameer. You have been a good student and a good professional. Now it's the time to be a good husband too," persuaded my mother.

"Mom, let me enjoy my free life," I said like other boys.

"Look, Sameer, please don't think marriage spoils your freedom. A true relationship sets you free."

I was overwhelmed by this. I purposely twisted the topic to avoid this confrontation now. "Ok, Mom, I will tell you if I like someone. Happy?"

She smiled and happily served me another helping. Sometimes lies save you. I heaved a sigh of relief. But I knew this was temporary. One or the other day, I will have to face her.

After that day, my mother started suggesting profiles of elligible brides to me. Later, she managed to convince my father, and even he sometimes asked me if I already had a girl in my life. My parents were okay with me marrying a girl of any caste. But what they wanted was to get me married soon.

I always wondered how their reaction would be when I would tell them I want to marry someone of the same gender! I had no option but to answer their every question with one, single reply, '*I need more time*'.

They ignored my reluctance as they knew well that boys and girls of our generation married late, and it was obvious that I would like to enjoy my life alone.

This was not going to stop here. I knew them well that they would bring out the same topic again and again. There was no way out but to confront them with my sexual orientation someday. Before I did that, I also needed to know about my future with Tanmay, so I would be able to mould my talk with my parents accordingly.

There was some progress in our relationship but not enough to conclude anything concrete. I knew he liked me, but that was not enough. I was no longer that childish Sameer who would keep on justifying every act of Tanmay. I had started noticing what others had noticed about him. Though I avoided answering the doubts of my friends, they did not leave my mind. I knew I had to give it some outcome. We had gone for a couple of treks when he had come to Pune. We had spent a great time at malls, sightseeing, and a wonderful bedtime too. But the moment I had steered my topic towards 'us' he had always changed it. We shared jokes on homosexuality and other dirty stuff, but that time it had a friendly touch and nothing of that sort. The only reason I did not push him towards it was I had noticed our bond getting stronger, and I wanted him to feel he is in love with me rather than me pushing him towards it. Though I was being overly optimistic, somewhere, I had an extreme fear of rejection. So, I had decided to treat it as a test of our love because I always believed that true love wins.

29

Preeti and I

Long back in my tenth, after Preeti completed my maths syllabus, she got married and left for the US. Later, I got busy with my SSC exams and lost touch with her. I had got my first mobile during my engineering days. I remember texting my mobile number to her. But she was so busy with her new beginnings that she hardly kept in touch with me. Unfortunately, by the time I joined my engineering college, she went through her divorce. So that was the time we got closer as she found more time for me. Lonely Preeti was trying to fill the vacuum in her life. That was the time we reconnected and became friends.

When we started chatting, I realised I had never seen her like this before. I could not accept that Preeti I knew was so different now. This divorce had sucked out life in her. She had become aloof and disinterested about everything she liked. I had never seen her in tears before, and I wanted to see her smile all the time. I always cared for her and comforted her in every way I could. I went out of my way to make her happy. I wanted her to share and empty her emotions which she had suppressed deep inside her. Whenever she felt lonely, she chatted with me. Sometimes even during my engineering exams, I chatted with her day and night to ease her emotional pain. I was there for her anytime to make her smile with my silly jokes. My life felt happier when she smiled. I don't know why but I cared for her more than any other friend in my life. As years passed, the seven-year age difference seemed to diminish. As we got closer, our friendship began to heal her stinging wounds. I wanted to help her, support her, and give her hope that she had a bright future ahead. I knew she was a very loving, warm heart and could keep any man happy.

Though she shared her emotional highs and lows with me, I was reticent when it came to my emotional life. Had I told her the details about Tanmay's behaviour, even she would raise doubts about his intentions like my gay friends. So, I spoke everything except that. She always stood by me like a real friend and mentored me when I had to deal with tough times.

One day, my father saw me engrossed chatting on my mobile, and he asked, "Whom do you chat with day and night, Sameer?"

"Preeti, dad."

"Sameer, I have seen you chatting with only one, single girl in your life. Your mother keeps on saying that she is your last-birth-sister, but I doubt," he winked!

"You have no other female friends who are that close," he added.

"See my boy, we are also okay if you love a girl who is elder to you. Though your mother is insistent on marrying a girl of the same caste, you know I am liberal about inter-caste marriages as well!"

He gave me one of his most understanding smiles. Don't hesitate to tell us if you like her. If you want, I can convince your mother."

"No way, dad! She is just a very good friend of mine!" I said.

"Hmmm, just friends?" he teased in a singy-songy tone.

"Sameer, are you hiding your feelings just because she is a divorcee? See, I know her well, she is a nice girl. We have no issues with this status of hers, and I don't think even your mother will have any. If she does, I can manage her," said my dad.

I started laughing out loud, "Dad, what's wrong with you? She is friend-zoned, dad. You are cracking the biggest joke in my life. I have no feelings for any girl, and Preeti is like my buddy dad. I share every little thing with her, but our bond is different."

Nothing surprising that my father felt this. He had heard me speaking to her for endless nights when she used to be disturbed after her divorce. Perhaps, it was that night that made my father think so.

One day, when Preeti saw Rohan with his second wife in a restaurant, she got very upset and called me that night.

"Sameer, I feel very upset after seeing Rohan with that girl. I find her no way better than me. Why did he leave me for her?"

"Preeti, it is always better to let go of the weaker relationships rather than holding on to them. It is good that you divorced before having kids," I said.

"I can't believe this. Our marriage had space, friendship, and trust. I see no reason for this to happen," said Preeti.

"The only reason was you were with the wrong person. Listen, life is a journey. Life partners are like our companions. They might be there with you during your journey or not. For some, there could be one life partner, and for others, it could be more. I have always thought of love and marriage more as a journey that begins when a couple commits to be partners. It continues till the moment when one of them takes their last breath or due to an unfortunate breakup of the relationship when they separate. Just remember and be happy with all that has enriched you. You still have a way long. Why not think about finding someone else?" I kept talking, and she was listening for a long time."

"I put my heart and soul in my relationship, Sameer. I made an effort to build a strong foundation of trust, and what did I get? I was cheated. I don't mind making compromises, but I should at least get some form of loyalty in return. For some, a marriage is an arrangement to have regular sex, for some, woman is a 'kids producing machine' for others, it is a an arrangement to get regular sex, while for some, it is a so-called ideal arrangement by our culture with some unrealistic expectation where the woman has to give up things. There are very few who understand the real essence of co-life. Rohan was among those few, but he cheated on me," and she started crying helplessly.

That night I remember counselling her for almost four hours in the night. My father had asked me the next day to whom I was speaking that night. This also happened but many times later. But I wished they knew I was gay.

30

The heartbreak

Hi Pri!

My company is finally sending me to Germany!

Only you know how desperately I had been trying to get an opportunity to go on a business trip there.

Even like last time, there was a discussion to send someone to the US. I was praying to God that it shouldn't be me!

Thankfully, he listened to my prayers, and the US project went on hold. Last week we had some clients from Germany with whom we needed to resolve certain issues and cater to their customized needs.

Whatever the reason was, somehow destiny opened the door for me.

You have no idea how happy I am!

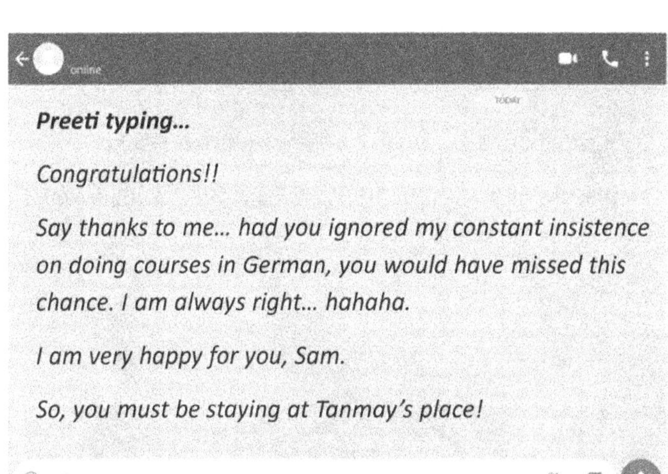
online
Preeti typing...
Congratulations!!
Say thanks to me... had you ignored my constant insistence on doing courses in German, you would have missed this chance. I am always right... hahaha.
I am very happy for you, Sam.
So, you must be staying at Tanmay's place!

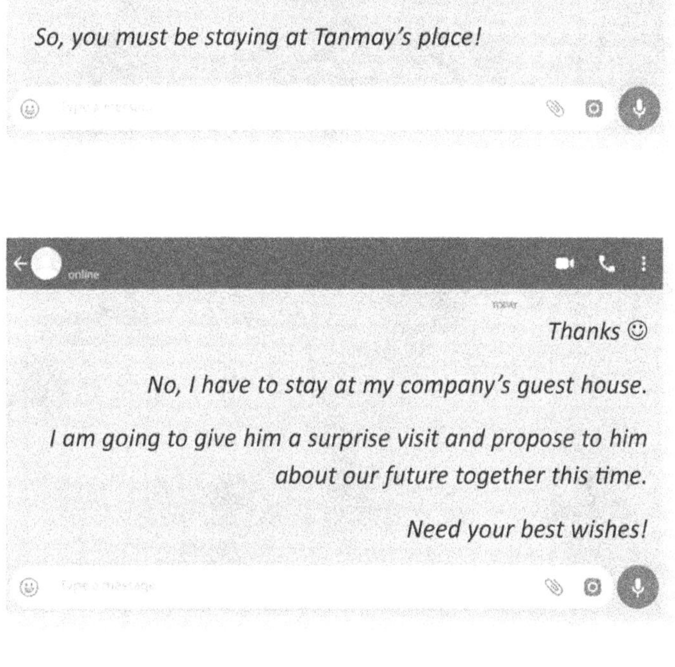
online
Thanks ☺
No, I have to stay at my company's guest house.
I am going to give him a surprise visit and propose to him about our future together this time.
Need your best wishes!

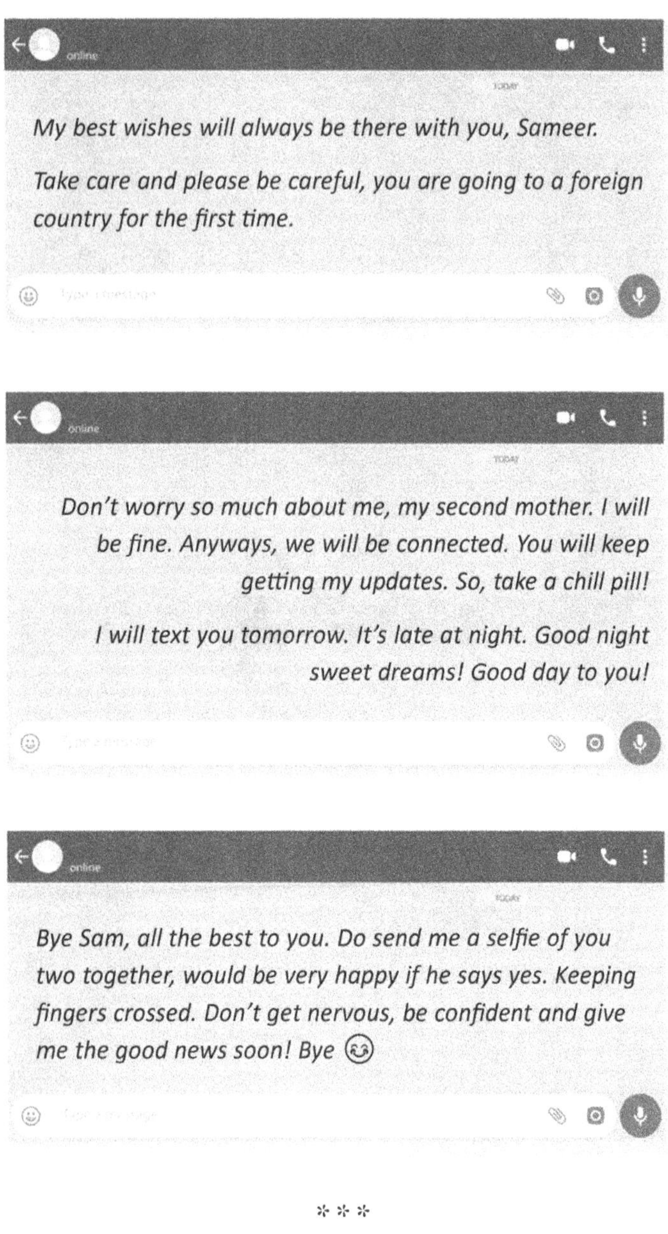
online
My best wishes will always be there with you, Sameer.
Take care and please be careful, you are going to a foreign country for the first time.
online
Don't worry so much about me, my second mother. I will be fine. Anyways, we will be connected. You will keep getting my updates. So, take a chill pill!
I will text you tomorrow. It's late at night. Good night sweet dreams! Good day to you!
online
Bye Sam, all the best to you. Do send me a selfie of you two together, would be very happy if he says yes. Keeping fingers crossed. Don't get nervous, be confident and give me the good news soon! Bye 😊

* * *

This was the first time I was travelling to a foreign country. After an exciting journey by Lufthansa, I finally landed at the German airport.

Everything was different here. I was very thirsty, needed water, so I tried to ask a man standing beside me, '*Wasser?*' and he pointed in the direction where drinking water was available. Nobody spoke without any reason. There was pin-drop silence at the airport. People only smiled at each other, and those who spoke were very soft-spoken. There was an old woman with a fair, freckled face dressed in a pearl white shirt and buff trousers. She was standing beside me, waiting for her luggage. There was another tall young man walking with his beautiful wife hand in hand. Everyone was busy in their own world. I found the culture very different here. The weather felt cold, the washrooms, though small, were super clean, and overall, it was less crowded. I wanted a sandwich but decided to skip it, looking at the price.

It was Monday morning, and I had to figure out things. The very first thing I had to do now was to reach my company guest house. I contacted Mr Müller, who was going to help me out with the whole thing. He picked me up from the airport, and we headed to our destination. I was seeing and observing things around, but my mental chatter kept me preoccupied.

I remembered I hadn't informed my mom, dad and Preeti regarding my safe landing. I quickly texted on our WhatsApp group '*Home*' and then Preeti, '*Reached safely*' with a selfie. I was around 5 hours ahead of Preeti's time, so it was unlikely for her to reply. I was on the way to my company guest house.

During all this while, Tanmay's thoughts ran in the background. I had purposely decided to meet Tanmay on Saturday and Sunday and then come back to India. I always had a habit of delaying the day of judgement and the results. It took care of my nervousness.

Tanmay's thoughts were constantly distracting me from the well-planned infrastructure and architecture in this new country. I was travelling on ultra-clean, busy roads, short houses with rooftops, I could see beautiful trees and flowers, but they slipped out of my eyes. Though I was in a beautiful country, my heart lingered in Tanmay's thoughts. I felt like sharing my selfie in the German cab as my WhatsApp status and check-in at Germany airport, but then I thought Tanmay would find out, and my surprise would fail.

Mr Müller, who did not speak much during our journey, dropped me at the guest house with a smile and goodbye. The company guest house was decent and comfortable. It was a super clean, posh place. It was just like any decent room in a posh hotel in India. I placed my luggage in the cabinet, changed into trousers and tees, and took a short nap.

When my eyes opened for a moment thought I am in Pune, but then I was finally here in Germany. I had to reach my office on time. So I rushed for a bath and left venturing through a metro. The scenic beauty visible during the travel was breathtaking. The lush green fields, a stretch of meadows, and beautiful trees calmed my eyes. There was a man next to my seat reading a book, but he did not look around. I tried to smile at him, and he smiled back but said nothing. I felt very lonely in this new country. After I reached my office, I met my team and got my workstation assigned.

The view from my office window was super scenic. But every now and then, my mind drifted away, searching for Tanmay, imagining us together in this heavenly place. I could not resist the temptation to send a WhatsApp to Tanmay that I am here, but I had to.

During my stay, I tasted various types of bread, cheese croissants and enjoyed eating other special cuisines of Germany. I was a bread lover, so the food here was a treat to my palate. I wondered how this country would feel if I settled with Tanmay here. My thoughts took romantic flights for no reason. But suddenly, I reminded myself, '*his response is yet to come.*'

The five days in the office were so hectic that after I immersed myself in work, I hardly got time to think about Tanmay or even enjoy my stay in the new country. I sincerely focussed on my work to finish the necessary feedback meetings with the clients. After catering to their expectations well, I was finally done and wrapped up on Friday.

Now I was looking forward to meeting Tanmay. I decided to give a surprise visit to Tanmay's home. I had brought a few gifts and a greeting card to express my love for him. I wanted to make him feel loved and special. On Friday night, his thoughts did not let me fall asleep.

***

I woke up, and the first thing I did in the morning was texting him, just to make sure he was home. I was super happy to see him online!

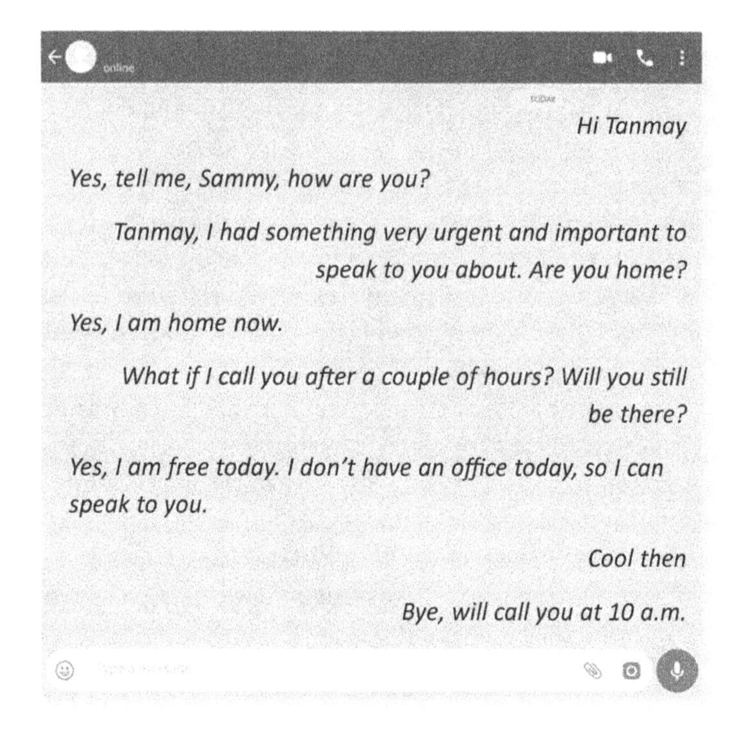

I was so happy to see Tanmay was free. I was nervous, excited, anxious, and eager. My mixed feelings fluttered in my tummy. I put on the best pair of clothes I had and waited for one of my German colleagues. Charles, who stayed nearby, had promised me to drop me at Tanmay's place.

After I reached his home, I rang the doorbell. A German man of an average height opened the door. He had silky, long hair tied up in a ponytail, had a fair complexion, and blue eyes. The moment I saw him, a horrible premonition suffocated me.

What was a man doing at Tanmay's place? He had never mentioned to me that he had roommates.

He always told me he stayed alone. A string of thoughts started bothering my mind making me paranoid.

"Hi! I am Sameer, from India. Is Tanmay at home?" I asked, gulping down all my fear. "Ah! Yeah, you are his brother, right? He once told me about you. No, my friend, he would be coming soon. Please be seated and make yourself comfortable."

I could not believe Tanmay had lied to me. My muscles felt weak after seeing this man here. I felt tingling all over my body and felt breathless. I was about to panic. After some time, my eyes caught the view of the bedroom. Sitting on the couch, I could see a double bed and felt even more anxious. When I looked around, the picture in the house showed that two people lived there. There were two slip-ons, two jackets, and a dining table for two. Now I was sure of one thing, this man stayed here. My paranoia had reached its height. I felt like running away from that place. But now, it was more important to find out. I had to be patient and trust my love. Maybe he could just be a roommate. I felt jealous of him and sensed an intense pain in my heart.

Upset with my negative thoughts, I tried to justify him. I thought, maybe all this could be false. Maybe he had recently shifted with a new roommate. Just the way I shared a brotherly bond with my gay friends, even he could be just friends with this man. Not all relations were based on sexual interests. I tried to gather my shattered hopes.

After some time, that German man came out and said, "I am getting late. I have to leave. Tan will reach within fifteen minutes. He has gone out for a walk." He took a sling bag lying down on the couch and hung it across his shoulders, and left humming some song.

I waited, counting minutes. The clock ticked slowly. After twenty long minutes, the bell rang. The pressure building up in my mind had left no confidence in me.

Tanmay opened the door, and the expression on his face calmed my upset mind.

"Oh my God, Sameer!! How come you are here? I can't believe my eyes! Is this a dream or something? Oh, pinch me, bro. How come you are here? I was expecting your call, and you teleported yourself or what?"

And he was overjoyed, and the bliss of meeting me had lit up his eyes and face. My face gained colour with this reaction. It was evident that if Tanmay did not panic seeing me here, he shared no such relation with that German guy.

I blushed and said, "I wanted to give you a surprise!"

"Sam, this was really the best surprise of the year!" exclaimed Tanmay patting on my arms.

"My company sent me here for a week," I added.

"You were in Germany for five long days, and I had no idea?" he said. I felt he was somewhat hurt.

"Why didn't you inform me before? I would have come to pick you up at the airport and would have invited you to stay at my place."

Hearing this, even the small remnants of my paranoid thoughts flew away from my mind leaving a confident smile on my face. This meant my mind had been making up stories. If that guy were Tanmay's boyfriend, why would he want me to stay at his place? So his openness was an indication that there was nothing between them.

He kept his water bottle in the kitchen and gave me a sudden warm hug, and said, "Anyways, your surprise made me happy!

With a spurt of excitement, I held his hug tightly and said, "I missed you so much, dear." Tanmay was taken aback by my unexpected, overly emotional gesture. Tanmay tried to loosen my hug and said, "Wait, let me get you a coffee. I know you like it. What else would you like to have?"

"Just coffee, please!" I started taking out the gifts from my sack. When Tanmay came out with two mugs of black coffee, he handed one to me. We started chitchatting about my agenda to come here. I looked deep into his eyes. I felt so happy we were together again and perhaps forever together. I unchained my sack and took out a paper that was rolled up with a red ribbon.

"Tanmay, I have something for you."

Tanmay kept his coffee mug on a small table, and he unrolled the paper. He saw his pencil sketch on it, which had my name written at the bottom.

"Lovely Sammy, this is so amazing. I can't believe my eyes. You are such a gem!"

I was overwhelmed by his reaction, and I took out a few sweets I had brought from India and some spicy snacks he liked.

"Hey Sameer, why did you get all these things for me?" he asked.

"Thank you, Sammy. You are such a darling."

That one word blew away all those pessimistic thoughts pestering my mind. My heart now pounded louder. I felt more confident after his positive reaction. One try was worth this visit. I tried to suppress my anxiety.

Then I took a red coloured paper bag handed it over to him.

"Please open it."

He opened the gifts. The first was a photo frame with a collage that had photos of us. He smiled and thanked me politely.

Then it was time to open the greeting which said those 3 special words 'I love you'. He opened it curiously and was shocked.

"What kind of joke is this, brother? Are you okay?" saying that, Tanmay burst out in laughter. I kept on looking at his face as my eyes were brimmed with tears.

Hearing these words, I went into a state of shock. I was not prepared for this. I felt numb now. He spoke out the truth that shattered my heart into pieces.

"Hey bro, what's wrong with you? We are brothers, aren't we? What is this love card for? How did you assume that I love you? Did I ever tell you that I love you? Didn't you realise that the man whom you must have met today is my boyfriend? Then where does this 'I love you' come into picture?" he said, letting out his disgust.

I was speechless after his reaction. I sank on the couch. I felt as if someone was sucking out my energy, and my legs had become paralysed.

I felt very humiliated. I spoke softly,

"Tanmay, what were those nights and days that we spent together? Wasn't it love? What about those surprise kisses and our lovemaking? Then why did you visit India so frequently? What about our trips and dates together?"

Tanmay looked at me as if I were babbling.

"Wait... what are you talking about? That was my need, your need, our body needs, and we both got pleasure. If you talk about the time we spent out, I did it because I like your company. You are my brother, and we share a wonderful connection. Please don't take it otherwise. I like you as a brother, and if it is for sex, I still don't mind doing it. And yes, my boyfriend whom you met knows it all. "

I asked, "If I am your brother, if that was not love, then what was that we did all the nights?"

Tanmay replied, "What I did to you was just out of my need, and even my boyfriend knows about it. Even he has had flings like this before. There is a vast difference between love and lust, and you misunderstood our fling for love. Did I ever tell you that I loved you? It was you who tried to speak some sentimental stuff with me, but I never encouraged such conversations."

"I never expected that you had been thinking of me as a life partner for so many years. Hey, you are my cousin! Have you lost your mind?"

I started weeping, and perhaps he took some sympathy on me. He sat beside me and put an arm around my shoulder.

He tried to speak softly now. He said, "Listen, for me, love and lust are two different things I underline again. I never gave you any emotional indication or misguided you purposely. I was born and brought up in a foreign country. My ethical and moral mindset is different from yours. It was my mistake that I did not realise it. I went with the flow. You never asked me directly, so I avoided telling you as I thought it would create a grudge between us. It was you who kept thinking that way. Come on, forget that shit and give me a nice hug like a brother."

I was broken and my dreams shattered. His words bled me. My heart was torn into pieces. The avalanche of disillusionments devastated me completely. I was immature to let all this happen. It was my mistake because I dwelled in dream worlds and never thought that reality would be so painful and unacceptable. But now, I had to blame no one but myself. Despite repeated warnings and heads up given by my friends, I preferred to ignore them and continue with my own plans. I had spent all these years in a fool's paradise, searching for some hollow hope.

I felt like Tanmay, and his boyfriend belonged to some other world. I was totally baffled. The memories of midnight flashed in front of my eyes, and I could not comprehend and process what was happening to me.

I thanked Tanmay for the coffee and requested that I would leave as I am not able to digest all of this at the moment. I needed some space and time to get over it. I left Tanmay's home, taking away my gifts and my bag. The words of Tanmay had hit me hard. I felt broken, cheated, and exploited.

* * *

I landed at Pune international airport. For all this while, I had not texted anything to Preeti, for I had always ignored her probing questions and never discussed anything about us with her. I knew what she was going to say. I simply did not want to face her, but one corner of my heart said, I wanted to speak to Preeti.

Now I could feel how she must have felt when she divorced. During my flight back to India, I typed out the whole story, and the moment I switched on the flight mode, I pressed enter.

I knew well that the moment she would read it, she would call me. I was waiting for her. I wanted to empty my heart. I could not tell this to my parents. I could not tell this to my gay friends too, for they would surely say it's the result of my ignorance. I had to digest this on my own. The only person who could understand my mistake was Preeti.

After six hours, there was a ping on my mobile.

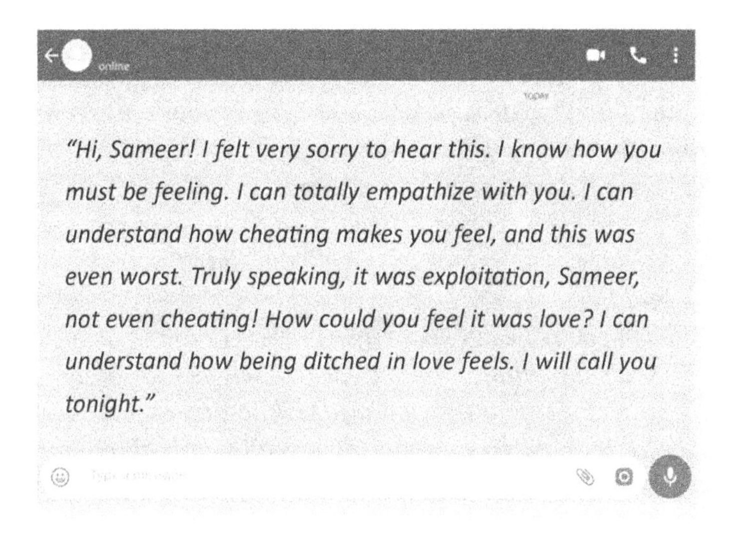

* * *

Preeti calling

"I don't know what to say. I can't believe Tanmay exploited you. If only you could have shared more about your relationship. I would have definitely sensed something was fishy," said Preeti.

"I repent for not sharing about my relationship with you. Preeti, here we are sailing in the same boat. You married in the most ideal way, and I lived an unrealistic dream, but we both ended getting nothing but pain. I have lost trust in true love and genuine relationships," I aggrieved.

"The silver lining of our relationship is that we both had each other when our love took a toll on us," Preeti said optimistically. "Time will heal you. It has great power. Just be patient. You never know you might even find someone!" added Preeti.

"Look who is saying that. I am going to give up thinking of love, and I am thinking of going for some blind dates," I declared. "Your case is different from mine. Something good might happen to you. There is always a balance of happiness and sorrow in life. Why indulge in such things?" Preeti tried to assuage me.

"Alright, tell me then why you didn't remarry?" I asked her.

"Sameer... I have lost trust in the goodness of men and their intentions. Some treat women as just another ATM machine if they earn well, while others feel she's a baby factory. How many men really care about the desires, emotions, aspirations, and dreams of women? I don't want to live another charmless marriage full of compromises and no emotional gains," Preeti burst out like olden times.

"I feel similar, but I do want physical gains, unlike you. That is why I have decided to join some dating site," I firmly said. "This is wrong. Don't enter this meaningless world of short term pleasures. It will lead you to nothing," she justified.

"Please don't advise me. Did you listen to me when I asked you to remarry? No, so why ask me to do anything that you feel is right? Bye, I am too sleepy, will call you later. I am jet-lagged. Good night"

I disconnected the call rudely.

31

The forbidden

After spending enough time licking my own wounds, I was ready to vent off the frustration simmering inside me. The rejection was giving me pain, and my physical needs were growing. The stress building in me caused so much distress that I felt the only way to forget my past is to get into multiple new relationships. The memories of his touch were engraved on my soul. I wanted to erase them, and the only way out was to create new ones.

So, one day, I signed up on 'Grinder', a dating app for gays. I uploaded the best photo I had. It highlighted my face and my slim fit structure of the body, very much visible from the skin fit t-shirt and jeans. I looked radiant with confidence. This picture was clicked one year before my breakup.

I signed up and signed in. I conveyed my interests to some and logged out. After some time, I received an interest from a handsome, decent man. Moderately built, he had spectacles, seemed intelligent and was a doctor by profession.

I was impressed. We chatted for a couple of days, discussing our sexual preferences and fantasies.

We met at decent restaurants a couple of times. We were okay to go ahead. We stayed in Pune, and to keep this a secret from our families, we decided to meet up at Mahabaleshwar, a famous hill station in Pune. He picked me up from my home in his red sedan. He wore an olive-green t-shirt, black jeans, and brown shades. He wasn't wearing his spectacles today. He opened the door for me with a sweet smile, and we drove to Mahabaleshwar. We had booked a nice three-star hotel for a night stay.

He seemed more than a hook-up date for me. We discussed our families, shared interest in astrology, art, and travelling; our talks were never-ending. I was disappointed to find out that he was married out of family pressure and had two kids. I had started looking at him as a prospective long term boyfriend, but by the time we reached Mapro garden, he had revealed his family status. That moment itself, I knew this was going to last just for a night or a few more, but had no chances to turn into nothing permanent.

He was polite, courteous, humble, rich, and intelligent. His wife was gorgeous, and he had two cute kids, one boy and the other girl. He was a 40-year-old doctor attached to all good hospitals in Pune. It was indeed a story of pain. He poured his heart out and said that he will be friends with me later and that I should not expect any more. Our night was great; he wanted hard-core sex, whereas I wanted foreplay. But he settled to my expectations. He was caring, adjustable and flexible. I badly wished he should have been single so that I can think of him for a long term. But there was a huge dead end there.

That night was very erotic. Later, we met again, many times that year. I was simultaneously dating many other men too. No one was really as good as him. Some dates stopped at McDonald's and Starbucks, while some ended at JW Marriot when it came to rich guys. Other dates were in some lower-middle-class homes and some in the outskirts of Pune. Some stopped at the coffee tables, while others ended up on the bed. Some memorable erotic adventures while some boring dates with no outcomes. These romantic adventures gave me a treasure of good, bad, weird, repulsive, romantic, erotic, and pleasant experiences. I came across a variety of people that made me see more of life. I also faced disillusionments and risky times.

Dates were always exciting when they began. When I returned home, I felt the hollowness and the vacuum in my heart pinching me. I felt trapped in this vicious cycle of lust. My way of forgetting my past had turned into an addiction to me. After every memorable make out and night strand, I felt extremely lonely and depressed. I felt a strong need to love and to be loved. Sexual errands did not satisfy my soul. I felt empty and vacant. How I wished I would find someone with whom I could share my soul. Someone who would be mine, and I would be his forever.

But after I returned home, I could not control the obsession I had developed. I wanted to share this tug of war in my mind with Preeti. But my ego stopped me from confessing it to her.

So, these sexual adventures went on until one day, it was not very long that my family found out 'the forbidden'.

32

Changed equations

Sameer's WhatsApp dropped a bombshell. The way he had narrated his story had given me a different picture of his relationship with Tanmay. But his text revealed a different face of their relationship. Had I been more probing, I could have easily found out this fact. I could have shown a red alert to Sameer then. Had I done it, it could have saved his numerous years of yearning.

After Sameer returned from Germany, he kept in touch with me all the time about how he missed Tanmay. He constantly kept on asking me if he could call Tanmay once and say sorry. I pitied Sameer, poor soul, I thought; despite being exploited, it was he who wanted to apologize and that too for confessing his love. Many times, I brainwashed his plans to contact Tanmay again and made him promise to me that he will not show a trace of sorrow even when he meets again. I forced him to wear the mask of brotherhood and move on. I stood by him and gave him enough strength to keep the promise he gave me. I had to make sure he comes out of this breakup marsh. He had always been there for me day and night when I was fighting my loneliness after my divorce. Though he was younger than me, he had warmly, lovingly consoled my heart and dressed my wounds. It was my time to make sure he survives this big blow. His love was ten years old and was not easy to forget. The memories he had about Tanmay were not erasable; they were trapped deep down in his mind. Though he wasn't there in a relationship, the bait of physical intimacy and moments spent together had added to his longing. It was his immaturity and romanticism that had caged him in an addictive relationship. He had tried suppressing his emotions, but it was a vent that he needed now. He had told me about his decision to start dating men. I had strongly opposed to which he had paid no heed. I was wondering in what direction was the ship of his life going to sail.

Frustrated and ditched by Tanmay, the equations in Sameer's life had totally changed. I had never imagined that he would really do what he had said in frenzy. A simple, innocent, honest, loyal boy turned into someone different. I could not see this happening.

After a call in the night which he had rudely disconnected, he sent me a message.

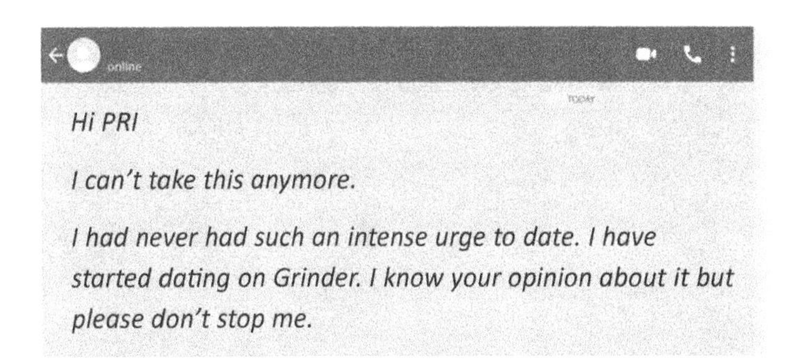

Lust was never a thing that haunted me, but now I can't control it anymore. I think doing this will help me forget Tanmay if I have more enjoyable experiences with others.

Please don't stop me, criticize me, or even judge me.

I did not reply to his message immediately. Something in me brought immense pain. I could not understand why his flings were upsetting me. I would have either convinced him not to do so, argued or fought for the better but, why did I feel hurt? I was too drained emotionally to reply to his messages but could not hold my emotions back.

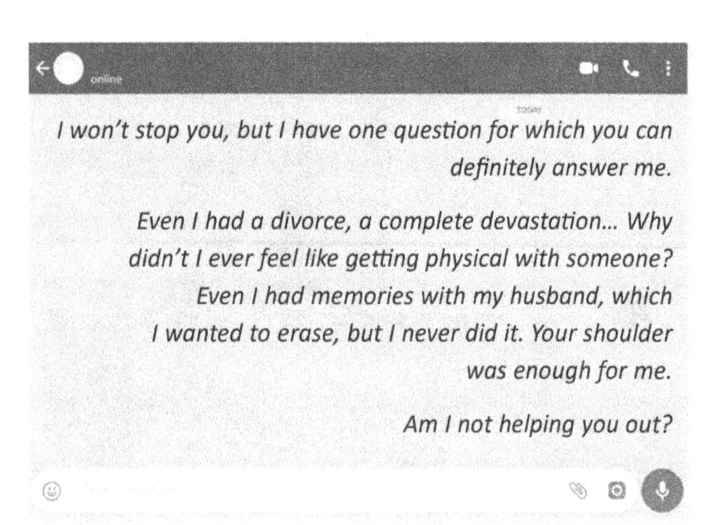

He was awake, and he replied to me,

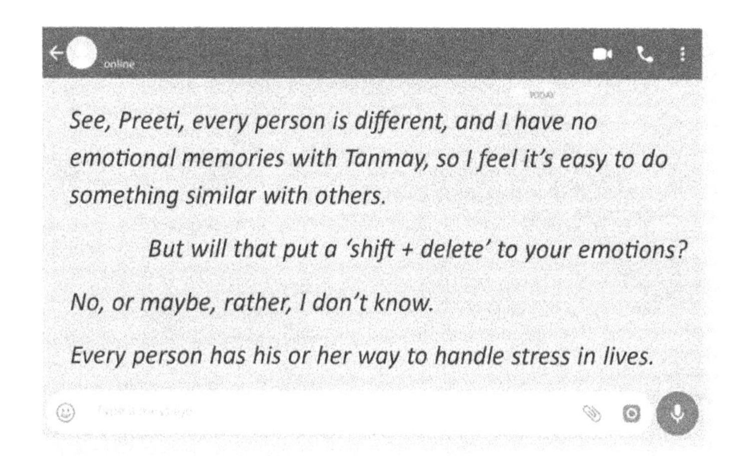

I felt dejected and could not believe this was happening to me. Was I falling in love with him? If yes, this was the greatest mistake I was making. He was gay, after all. What was I thinking? He was never going to think of me that way.

When he had told me about his relationship, I never got jealous or sad. On the contrary, I was very happy that he had someone in his life. I could not believe that I had started feeling for him so intensely after his heartbreak. I could not control my emotions for him. The way this realization had cropped up all of a sudden had shocked me.

Was it because he looked similar to Rohan? Was my friendship with Sameer a rebound relationship? Maybe, unknowingly, I had tried replacing my emotional relationship with Rohan with Sameer. When I came to know that the boy who once dreamt of having meaningful deep love started looking out for hook-up dates, I felt like a loser. I realised that though he got affection and emotions from me, I was not of any use for him when it came to sexual pleasures. Why? Because I was a woman. Today I wished I were a man.

He started spending hours together on dating sites and chatting with random men online.

I could see him online, but at times, he said, "*TTYL, I am chatting with some handsome hunk. Catch up with you later.*"

This was very painful for me. I sailed through more painful moments. I tried becoming more social to deal with this and distanced myself from Sameer. He was more into dating and meeting guys than sharing anything with me. This went on and on. He was not the kind of a man who would be into momentary happiness and fun. To get over his heartbreak, he tried and was trying to walk in the footsteps of Tanmay. However, I strongly believed that one day he will definitely get frustrated and come back searching for a meaningful life.

33
The confession

I was sitting in my living room, checking out some profiles on Grinder. Completely engrossed stalking a profile of a sexy man, I was unaware that my father was around. I did not realise when he stood behind me and peeped twice into my phone.

My father shouted, "Sameer... what are you doing? Give me your phone." He snatched it from my loose grip. I was startled and was not alert enough to close the chat window. "What you have been doing these days?" he shouted at me. His fair skin was red with anger. "Wait... let me check... what is it? Dating... what is this site?? inder... Tinder? Are you on Tinder? I can't believe this."

He had not seen that the profiles he was checking were of men and not women, and the word grinder had also slipped from his sight.

"No, dad, it is not tinder," I said, taken aback by his sudden invading my personal space.

"How easily you lie, my boy! My son, who once found lying difficult, is lying so effortlessly," he sarcastically said.

"I am not lying, dad," I said, feeling offended.

"Sameer, you know very well that I don't mind you having a girlfriend. You can get married to anyone whom you like. We are not so rigid about the caste and family background too. We are ready to accept your choice. But I will certainly not tolerate it if I find you dating random girls. This is completely unacceptable to me as well as your mom. We could have even been fine with a live-in relationship. At least it would have had some emotional grounds. If you continue with this, we are going to get you married at the earliest. Whatever you may label me, may it be an orthodox dad or a dictator. I don't care. I will certainly not let this happen. I am telling your mother about this right away. Just wait here," he said, getting even more furious than before.

The waterfall of his anger ended, and I tried to breathe. I could see the tall image of my father disappearing in the bedroom. His slouching shoulders were now lower with disillusionment. His anger was superficial, but at heart, he found this as his failure. I was terrified to confront my parents about these things. It was time for them to know the bitter truth. My father had never been so angry with me in my entire life. I felt very embarrassed. I knew how my mother would feel. Perhaps the only way to handle this situation was to tell them the truth.

I was so nervous and stressed that I could not think. Now I could hear my mother and father in the bedroom. I was terribly afraid to hear my usually calm and composed mother shouting. She sounded enraged. I had never seen her in this mood ever in my life. I could hear this conversation and see them speak vehemently. They were approaching the living room. Both of them had lost their temper. It was my time to panic now. I started searching for words.

Before they could speak, I decided to open up. "Dad, before either of you say anything, I want to tell you my story. After you listen to it, I will agree with anything you want me to do. But please listen to my side," I pleaded again.

"Mina, do you even think there is any point left in wasting our time talking to him?" he spoke out with frustration.

My mother looked broken and devastated. She was helplessly looking at my father with a deep concern in her eyes, "Sushant, what is this you have been telling me. I am completely shattered after listening to this. We had brought up our son with such great care and inculcated good ethics and morals. How can this be true?"

My father spoke with indignation, "I couldn't believe my eyes. It's good that I caught him red-handed. It was my mistake. You were right. We should have fixed him up with a girl. I shouldn't have let him free. But I am going to straighten him up now. He is taking undue advantage of our pampering, love and freedom."

My face was wet with sweat. I had gathered courage but had no words to tell them the facts. I closed my eyes and said, "Mom and Dad, till today, I have done every little thing you wanted me to. I have made your heads high with pride. But I will never marry a girl."

My father got up, and beckoning me, he said, "I will never let this happen. Till your mother and I are alive, we will never ever let you indulge in such things. We will start finding someone for you, and you will have to marry her or stay single. But I am not going to take this shit of your one-night stands ever again," he growled.

"I am ashamed to have a son like you. You are such a big liar. Even when I caught you on Tinder, you say it's not Tinder," his voice echoed in the living room.

I was very upset with his reaction. I was trying to control my emotional outburst. My mother interrupted his outbreak and said, "Sameer, what is wrong in marrying a girl? Why don't you want a stable relationship? Tell me, Sameer, what is the reason behind this thinking? You have been a deep thinker and never someone shallow who will find pleasure in such things. You have always preferred meaningful relations and things. What changed you so much?" she began weeping. Her anger had converted into sorrow seeing my firmness that she thought was adamance.

"Mom, it's not like I don't want a long-term relationship." I had already started yelling with desperation. My hands trembled and quivered while I spoke. "For gay like me, I don't think I can marry someone and settle down, but it's difficult to find a perfect match. What do I do? By the way, dad, I am on Grinder, a dating app for gays, and yes, I wasn't lying."

I had not realised that I had unknowingly mentioned what I was trying to hide for years long. A thing so difficult had become so easy to express during this heated conversation with my parents. My parents were dumbstruck by what I said. I could see it in their eyes that they were hurt. Even when none of them spoke a word. They kept looking at me with shocked faces. However, it was time to confront and convince them.

Listening to the word 'gay', my mother helplessly collapsed on the couch. My father kept looking at me with a frozen, expressionless face. Ignoring their reactions, I went on.

I boldly continued, "I groomed myself into a son you wanted. But today, the fact that I am gay will perhaps make you forget all good things I did till now." The words banged on their ears one more time. My voice had torn their eardrums. Their shocked eyes kept on staring at me for some time.

My mother was broken by this outbreak. Her initial reaction seemed better as compared to this. She appeared extremely devastated.

"*Beta*, how come it never struck me? Did I fail as a mother? Was I wrong to not allow you to have female friends? What made you go this way, *beta*? Where did we go wrong? Don't worry, you will be fine one day. You can marry any girl you want. I will have no restrictions, even about the caste or religion. But I pray to God to make you normal again," she said, sobbing.

My dad was so shocked that he was not able to digest this fact. After some time, his face started showing different shades of repulsion, disgust, hatred, hopelessness, disappointment, anger, and grief.

My mother continued, "Maybe if you marry a beautiful girl and love her, you will become normal, *beta*. But please don't do this. Did it happen because we restricted you from mingling with girls?"

"Mom, please don't say this. I know this is a huge shock but let me tell you, being gay is very much human, natural, and normal. There is nothing abnormal happening to me. There was nothing wrong with my upbringing on your or Dad's part. I am ready to do anything except for marrying a woman. I can't spoil the life of a woman. One of my gay friends was forcefully married to a woman, which spoilt both lives. She is going to file for a divorce. There is one more man I met during my dates, he is married to a woman. He has kids, so he cannot stay with me even though we liked each other. You can spoil my life but don't spoil the life of any other girl in this world. I won't be able to give her the love that she needs. Nothing can change me because God has made me this way."

My mother was in dismay. My father was still not in a condition to speak. The negative shade on his face seemed to mitigate now. Perhaps he regretted what he had said and perhaps he could not understand what to do. He seemed to be searching for words.

Before he spoke and I added further, "Do you remember, Dad, once an astrologist had told you after he saw my horoscope that your son will remain single forever? If that's true, sometimes, I feel why I shouldn't enjoy my life. A happy life is my right too!"

After a long time, he said, "It is difficult to accept this but fine, we can find some solution. I will take you to the best psychiatrist, and you will be fine."

"No, dad, I am fine. There is nothing wrong with me. I am not coming with you to any psychiatrist."

"Ok. We will discuss this later," he said in a very curt tone. "Well, I am getting late for my office, you go to yours. We will discuss it tomorrow."

I did not like his gesture. I didn't have a mental disease. That day, no one had breakfast properly. I silently had tea and left my home. My mother was lost in her own world and hardly spoke anything to my father or even me. My father, who never left for office without a heavy breakfast, left on a cup of tea that day. The whole day I was not at all attentive during my meetings and worked with almost no efficiency. The thoughts about the morning conversation constantly bothered my mind. I stayed back at the office for an extra couple of hours to finish my target and returned home. When I came back, my parents were out. My mother had texted me, *'the dinner is on the table. We will return late'*. This was odd. My parents never went out in the evening and never on working days.

I waited for them to return and then went to my room. Though I chatted with Preeti, I purposely avoided sharing with her about the catastrophe that morning, for I knew she would support them. But I wanted to ask her why my mother, who appreciated her for being an LGBTQ activist, could not accept that her son was gay. Why the sudden change when it came to her own son? She thought it was abnormal. But I avoided talking about the whole thing now.

After a couple of hours, I heard my parents enter the house. I dare not confront them. At midnight I stepped out of the room to refill my water jar. My mother and father were whispering in low voices. I wondered what it was that had kept them out the entire day. More importantly, awake at this midnight hour. The night was long, and I was doing nothing but killing time with mobile games. There was a time when I loved listening to music, doing creative stuff, sketching, but all had ceased after my heartbreak. The series of hook-ups that followed had sucked out the passion in my life.

* * *

The next morning none of us spoke to each other. I tried to spend most of the day out of the house. During dinner time, my parents did not speak to me. Everyone had dinner silently. Pressure had built up among us, and the openness had vanished. It suffocated me. A few days passed in a similar way. I was not able to withstand their silence. I felt like a criminal. I felt as if they hated me. I felt guilt and killing me. Two more days passed, and one fine morning sun shone brightly for me.

I brushed my teeth, finished my daily chores, and stepped into the kitchen, gathering strength. Though I was scared to confront them, I decided to break the ice. I saw my mother sidewise. She was not in a great mood. My father was sitting at the dining table with a cup of tea and a dish full of biscuits. He still looked annoyed.

"Good morning, mom and dad. I am sorry for the way I spoke to you that other day."

Nobody said anything. "Mom, dad, please forgive me."

My dad frowned and said, "Hmm."

"Let me not hide anything from you. It was a big shock for us. We took time to digest things. We went to meet Prashant this week, a friend of mine who is a psychiatrist. I wanted to understand and discuss about you." *'Why he even did that?'* I thought. But it was also their right to do a bit of research to understand things.

"He told me all about physical and psychological aspects of the third gender and especially gays. I wanted to know whether we had been at fault for you being this way," saying this, he exhaled.

"So, what did Prashant uncle say?" I asked with curiosity.

"Nothing, he said we can't help it in your case. It is just natural, and we better accept it as you did," my father replied coldly.

"Hmm," I said, thanking God in my mind. "See, we discussed a lot about the whole thing. Your mom is still in the process of accepting things, and so I am."

My mom brought three plates of *Upama*, and we started eating. She did not say a word. But the good part was my father was speaking to me. Now I wanted to listen to my mother's voice. I knew what the shock had done to her, and she seemed broken. She remained silent and kept cursing herself for things. This was how my mother was.

"We can now try to think about things from your point of view. But you understand us and our side as well. Suppose we accept that you are gay and even try to help you when you need it... will you promise to stick to one partner?" asked my dad.

"Ok, dad, I will do as you say. I am deeply touched by your effort to understand me," I spontaneously said.

My mother finished her breakfast and left us alone, assuming that we needed privacy.

"What do you do on these dating sites, my son? Isn't there a risk to catch AIDS? Even you may get contagious skin diseases."

"I regretted what I spoke that day, and I feel sorry about it. But I still have a fear of you ending up having AIDS. No father can ever live with this fear. I understand and empathize with all that you have gone through, but..."

I interrupted his talk, "Well, dad, I really don't like hardcore activities. I just indulge in foreplay. There is no risk of AIDS in that case, and I have always taken good care and enough precautions."

"Whatever, but I really don't like this. We have brought you up with good ethics and morals. Your mother and I have always been loyal to each other. We also expect you to do the same with your partner. Had you been straight and have done the same, I would have taken the same stand. And yes, I don't believe in horoscopes, so you better not use that as a shield. You might find someone in life."

"What about Preeti? Even she is divorced. She might have plans to get married or stay single, but does she do such things? I know she isn't that kind of girl."

I frowned, and he understood that I did agree with him.

"I wish I would have been with you when you suffered from ragging in your school days. I would have been a better father then. Though I couldn't do it then, I will try to do my role in a better way. I can imagine how it must have been for you to face all this alone."

"Well... even your mother wants to say something. Mina... please come... we have finished talking most of the things."

My mother came into the kitchen, wiping her forehead with her saree. She was actually wiping her tears while acting as if cleaning her sweat.

"Yes, *beta*, though it was difficult to digest the fact, I sincerely want to help you." She tried to control herself a lot, but tears flowed through her eyes. "Isn't that a good thing that you are gay? I will be spared from the daughter-in-law fights!" she said, trying to light up the mood.

"Well, tell me, when are you planning to get a son-in-law for me?" she said while trying to smile.

Their words melted my heart. I felt so guilty about the way I had behaved. I hugged my mother. How understanding my parents were! Did I really deserve this enormous support and love? Why was I being so adamant?

"By the way, Sameer, who all know you are gay?

"Well, my three friends from my school, Akash, Vivek and Pranit; Preeti and one more girl in my college, Nisha."

"Oh, they knew it? Aren't the boys worried that you may like them? He tried to crack a lame joke. My parents were trying to be friendly. Though their efforts sounded artificial, their intentions were genuine, and that sweetness gave me a very special warmth. "Dad, they are gays. We four are brothers, dad... we have no such feeling for one another," I said, raising my eyebrows and smiling sheepishly.

"What? How come so many gays in one school? This is unbelievable?" my dad was flabbergasted.

"Yes dad, no one knows that there are so many gays in this world and let me tell you that more than 10% of people in this world are not straight. This is what statistics say, not me."

"Alright, the better part of your story is you have friends who are like you."

"Well then, what about Nisha? Once or twice, I think I have heard this name."

"Yes, dad, she was in love with me. I feel sorry for her. I told her the truth, and she felt bad. We are no longer friends now."

"Oh Nisha, that cute girl in your class, I was under the impression you liked her," added my mother.

There were endless questions from that day. My parents were actively trying to take an interest in my life. They wanted to show how much they loved me. They wanted to compensate for my lonely years during school. After I went to my office, I kept thinking about what I was going to do with my dates. I had a couple of plans for next week; with one man from Delhi and the other from Calcutta. Both had come to Pune and started with new jobs. They were so hot and irresistible. I was so happy they had liked me. I didn't want to let go of that chance.

On the one hand, my parents were being so supportive, and on the other hand, I could not resist the temptation to break the promise I had given. So if I changed the passwords of my phone and started being more careful and cautious. I even started taking my phone to the washroom though usually, no one snooped in my phone.

Not just them, but I knew even Preeti did not like what I was doing. She felt that it was not right. But I had no option but to meet my needs, not just the lust of my body but also that need for appreciation and acceptance. I needed sex to deal with my insecurities and convince myself I was good enough to be chosen. I wanted to use it to clear my memories about Tanmay. But I could not tell this to my father. Though I said 'okay' on his face, I could not let go of the thought of continuing the whole thing secretly.

34

Sailing the rough sea

I was finding it very difficult to live my life on my parents' terms. I was not able to stay away from 'Grinder'. My dad had asked me to deactivate my account and turn my back towards this kind of life. The way my mother and father had faced this shock, I felt very guilty to cross the line they had drawn for me. The health concern they had for me was fair enough and made sense. But they could not step into my shoes and understand why I felt like taking this risk. They did not know about my heartbreak and why I was trying to go for hookups. They had no idea how deep Tanmay's memories were buried in my heart and how important it was to forget those. Dating helped me get out of it. This was my way to get out of the mess in my life. It was working quite well for me, so I had no reason to justify it to others. With this emotional dilemma going on in my mind every moment, I felt like crossing the line they had drawn for me every now and then. Suffocated with these thoughts, I texted Preeti,

Hi Preeti,

Sorry, I have not been in touch with you.

I am sure you must have guessed why.

Finally, my parents came to know I was dating, and I am gay. It is a long story. I will tell you about it later, but now they have drawn a line for me. I feel like crossing it all the time, but the way they have accepted my gender makes me feel highly obliged. I have no option but to accept their expectations too!

I know you would very much agree with them. You must be very happy to hear that. I really doubt how long I can follow these restrictions.

I still think creating new memories would help me forget old ones. That is the very reason I can't stay away from Grinder. I need to speak to you regarding this, whether you agree with me or not. Because I am sure, though our opinions may differ, you are the only one who can understand me. It has always been you who helped me get out of the mess I have always made in life.

Preeti, please call me asap, I need to speak.

She had read the message and had come online several times. I waited for her reply, but she did not respond. I felt very much concerned. Meanwhile, I had installed and uninstalled the dating app many times. It was getting tough for me, and I was feeling more and more confused. I was worried about Preeti. She had never done this to me before. I tried to call her, but she declined it. It was midnight, and I was awake only to speak to her. But she kept on rejecting my calls. I thought maybe she is occupied and tried to sleep.

After waiting for her for a long day, I got her reply

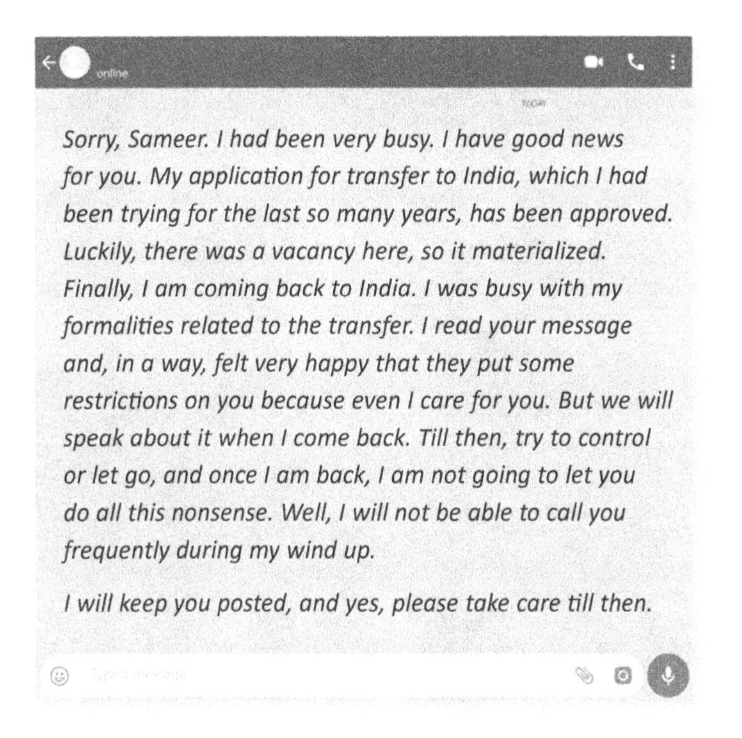

My happiness knew no bounds; I was dancing. "Yippee!! Preeti is coming back," I literally shouted out loud.

My mother stepped inside, hearing me yell, and asked, "Why are you so excited? What happened!"

"The good news is that Preeti is coming to India... finally..."

"I am happy that she is coming back. I am going to ask her to box your ears," said my mother in excitement.

"Whatever, mom, let her do what she feels like. I am just happy that she is coming."

Her single message was like a pleasant sunrise after a night full of nightmares. It did not matter whether she spoke to me or not, but the best part was that my loneliness was going to be over. I was overjoyed and slept well that day.

35

Crossing the line

"*Hi sexy, how are you, long time man, let's meet up.*"

I wish this text would have come up from Tanmay. But I had decided not to think about my past that badly ached my heart. I reminded myself that he had exploited me and did not deserve my love. This text was from Rock. We had enjoyed many erotic nights together. His one single message lit a fire in my heart. I lost my control and planned a staycation with him for two nights on the weekend. I had learnt to lie nowadays. So Rock and I went to JW Marriott. He was a wealthy businessman, and I was a middle-class guy. He knew I could not afford such expensive adventures, so he spent a lot of money on me. He gifted me branded clothes, watches, perfumes and whatnot. I was very happy and immersed myself in his intoxicating romance. Like many previous nights, we had a wonderful time together.

The next morning, I returned home with a guilty heart. When I came back home, my mother was in the kitchen. I tried to speak to her, but she kept mum. I thought maybe she is busy with something, so I did not think much about her. After some time, she went out, and I forgot about her behaviour. I opened my laptop and started working. I had a client's call and had to prepare for it. The hangover of the weekend had made me lazy. It was not only the effect of booze, but it was his charm that had stupefied my brain.

After some time, the effect of the night faded, and I started feeling bored, lazy, irritated, and guilty. I had contradictory thoughts. Why was everyone trying to control my life? Even Preeti wanted to, but I had drawn a line. I had spent my whole life living as per my parents' wish, but now I had decided to live for myself. What was wrong in making a few mistakes? Mistakes enrich you anyway. I had lived for my parents for more than half of my life and then in the hope that Tanmay would say yes one day. Though my parents wanted to help me out, they had no idea about the real pain burning my heart.

The day passed quickly, and the doorbell rang. I was relaxing on the couch of the living room.

"Hi, when did you come back?" I heard my father.

"Morning, dad!"

"Check your WhatsApp, son. I have sent you some nice photos of yours."

The moment I checked those on my WhatsApp, I started trembling. I could not believe my eyes. Those were my photos with Rock. So my father had caught me red-handed. How could I forget? My father often visited JW Marriot for his meetings. It was so careless of me. I had made such a blunder while getting carried away with Rock's charm. But one mistake was now going to bring me in trouble. I had no guts to face my father.

"You asshole, how could you do this? You don't deserve to stay in the house. Get out right now," he growled.

My mother stood away from us, feeling repulsed. Now I knew why she wasn't speaking to me. Somewhere at the same time, I felt I did not care about what they felt about me. Though I was frightened to confront my father's music, once upon a time innocent, I had become adamant.

"I told you in all possible ways if you cannot listen to me, get out of the house right now. You took undue advantage of my good behaviour with you," my father said furiously.

His voice shook me in and out, and again, I felt afraid of the tornado which was right over me now. I lost my poise and my politeness. I was trembling, freaking out, losing my control.

"I cannot follow your ethics. You have not gone through what I have. Don't expect me to obey you anymore. I want to live life on my terms."

Slappppp

My father slapped me on my face and very hard. The moment he slapped me, his face showed a light shade of regret. His anger calmed down, and he continued.

"Listen to me well, once and for all. We have been more understanding than you deserved. What do you mean when you say you have faced? Tell me, what pulls you in this dirty marsh of hook-ups? You can have a boyfriend, bring him home, and we will happily treat him like your spouse with all due respect and love. What else do you want?"

I was already upset with his reaction. Overcoming the turmoil in my mind, I spoke out loudly, "Dad, I madly loved someone for more than ten years, and he broke my heart. I got frustrated and... I started indulging in this to wash out his memories, and now it has become a vicious cycle... my anxiety first, then the need to vent it off and then these hook-ups."

My dad took pity on me. Though he lost his temper quickly, he calmed down quite soon. "Look, Sameer, I don't believe in restricting anyone's freedom. I respect your orientation, and I respect your choice of life. I have already told you that I will support you if you love someone. I am ready to accept him as an integral part of our family, just the way I would have done for a girl. If you have two or three men in your life during different times of your life, this is understandable. But if you start choosing a life with flings, you will meet men of similar lifestyles. It will increase the risk of serious diseases. Try to understand that I am asking you to stick to a single person in life only for your own wellbeing. It is also good for your emotional stability. Flings don't help you when you face a problem in life. You need a life partner to support you and help you grow. Fling helps you run away. Why cannot you understand my love and care behind my restrictions? My obedient son has turned so rebellious. I don't like it. When I respect your freedom, I expect you to behave with responsibility."

"Tell me today, who was the man who broke your heart and what has caused you so much pain. If necessary, let's go to a psychiatrist to overcome that pain. Don't try to wash out your memories with such flippant life," he spoke in a more understanding tone.

"If you tell me your story, maybe I can help to bring you both together again. But please stop this," said my father. His hand was around my shoulder, and I could see that he was trying to behave like a friend.

"Dad, if I tell you the story, I feel terrified that you might kick me out of the house," I said with hesitation.

"Even after all these episodes, I haven't disowned you yet. What more can take my anger to that level? Rest assured, you tell me what it is. Tell me all your worries, and we see how we can go ahead with your problems."

"See, I feel guilty every day for not being with you in that phase of teenage when you needed me the most. That was the time you needed our support, and I was not a keen observer to find it out. So, I feel I have made a mistake. So whatever mistakes you might have committed, I am equally responsible for it. So please feel free to share. I also promise you that I will not share it with your mother."

"Please keep it between us," I pleaded again.

"I will," assured my father.

I felt more comfortable and decided to open up.

"Dad, it was Tanmay, my brother!"

I narrated all the episodes with Tanmay, including sexual activities, but without explicit details. The story was another shock to him.

"Your life is a chain of shocks indeed. Oh my god! I had no idea Tanmay is gay too. So, did he force it on you and changed your orientation?" asked my father.

I was irritated with his words and said, "Dad, no one forced anything on anyone. Please don't blame yourself for this or even Tanmay. I was naturally gay. It was just that my interactions with Tanmay revealed why I was never interested in girls and why I liked being with boys. It had occurred to me many times that I get turned on by boys, but I regarded it as a mere coincidence. So please accept me the way I am. Don't start with the blame game of who spoilt me. I am not spoilt but hurt."

There was a long patch of silence. Finally, my father said, "Give me some time to think. This is too much together and so all of a sudden. I don't want to be an unjust parent and fuss about things thoughtlessly. I need time to comprehend your situation. Please stop these activities for now. We will surely find a way to deal with your breakup. Now it's not only your problem but ours too. Promise me that you will not indulge in such things anymore."

"Yes, Dad. I promise you. I am sorry."

"I had Preeti who understood such things. But after I told her about my hook-ups, even she has given me the cold shoulder."

The day went very smooth. After a long time, I felt very light. The onus on my heart had finally gone. At least, I could confront the real thing pinching my heart.

The next evening, my dad and I stepped out for a walk after he returned from his office. Dad wore smart sportswear today. He looked so young. At this moment, I felt there was no generation gap between us. I felt I had found a friend in him. I never wanted to disappoint him in my life.

"After all that you told me, I see there is no point in thinking about Tanmay. You need someone as a life partner and not someone who will be a partner to meet physical needs. You might find some nice, good-natured guy. Give it some time. If you want to forget those memories, create new, beautiful, touching moments with someone. See, marriages are made in heaven, if God is fair with you, you will definitely find the love of your life, and everything will be washed out. Please wait with patience."

"Yes, Dad, I get your point. But I have stuck to foreplay only. Don't worry; I have no risk of AIDS. I was still trying to convince my side, trying to get the boundaries loosened."

"All these pleasures are temporary, my son. Try finding something which is more valuable and more eternal."

I felt he was right. Maybe I was astray. I had to find a purpose in my life and get more focused. I could even work for the third gender community and for our rights. I had never thought in this direction. I could join Preeti's organization that works for the LGBTQ community and get more involved in something more meaningful. There are so many LGBTQ organizations in Pune. After Preeti comes to India, I can start with her; maybe I might find someone there, I thought.

We returned home after a heart to heart talk over a walk which made my day fruitful.

My focus in life was back after our talk. I suddenly realised how far I had gone from my friends due to these activities. I decided to reconnect with them that night.

I texted on our group 'Best buddies',

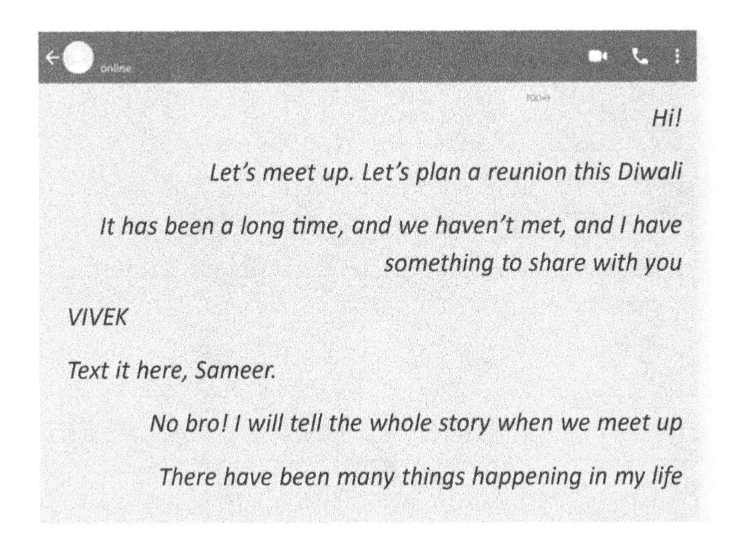

AKASH

I don't want to hear any suspense stories of yours. Let's have a group call now and talk about it. Are you all there?

(There were thumbs up from all)

PRANIT

Common Sam, you always have stories to tell, be quick and start.

We met on a video call then. I narrated the major incidents one by one, and I told the whole story beginning from my break-up, my friendship with Preeti, the confrontation with my father and the recent incident where my father became my friend. I felt better after sharing my emotions. Their lives had taken new turns too. Akash had found a boyfriend in Mumbai, and later, they both had settled in the US. Vivek and Pranit were single.

"Akash said, breakups are a part of life, dude, but you are lucky to have such an understanding father. I found Harry after having relationships with ten weird people."

Vivek said, "I always felt that your love was one-sided. It would have been better had you led a single life rather than doing this."

"When you all were busy, I fought this all alone. That was the time I met Preeti. Her marriage broke, and she was all alone, suffocating in her emotions. That was the time we became friends. She is an LGBTQ activist. The best part of my life now is she is coming to India."

"We are very happy for you," said Pranit; this means there is someone to take care of our little boy. You have no idea your life is heaven as compared to other homosexuals. You have supportive parents, one rock-strong friend, we and what not. You have a good job. What you lack is a partner for your life. When straight people don't find good partners so easily, how can we?

"You need to keep track of the number of men. You have become so vulnerable, Sameer. You shouldn't be that way. Doing hookups for hookups' sake is fine. But living such a life just to forget someone and run away from those haunting memories is very stupid. This kind of life isn't for you."

"By the way, we all would like to meet this friend of yours, Preeti. She seems to have a great influence on you," said Akash

"Sure."

Beep
The call got disconnected due to a network issue.

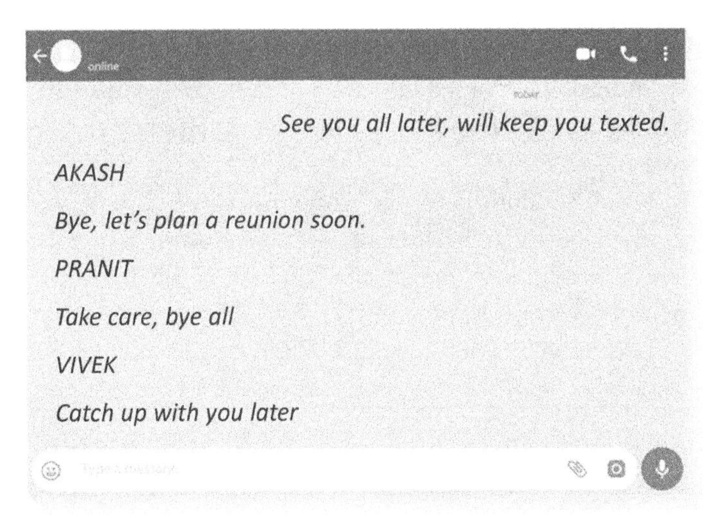

36

Back to Sameer

I had finally come back to my motherland. It had been years-long that I had been away from India. Bathing in the air of my motherland rejuvenated my soul. This is silly to hear from a US returned person, but yes, sometimes clean, fresh air makes you feel more suffocated with loneliness.

I had come back from a beautiful, clean, and technologically advanced country. But the picture of the Indian road full of potholes, stray dogs crossing the streets, busy *tapris*, and crowded *thelas* calmed my fatigued eyes. I reached my home and rang the bell. My mother welcomed me with a bone-breaking hug, planting a huge kiss on my forehead. I felt so warm in her arms.

"I am so happy to see you, my child. I will ask the maid to shift the luggage to your room. You take a shower and join me in the kitchen. Your favourite cuisines are waiting for you!"

I was tired and jet-lagged. I WhatsApped Sameer.

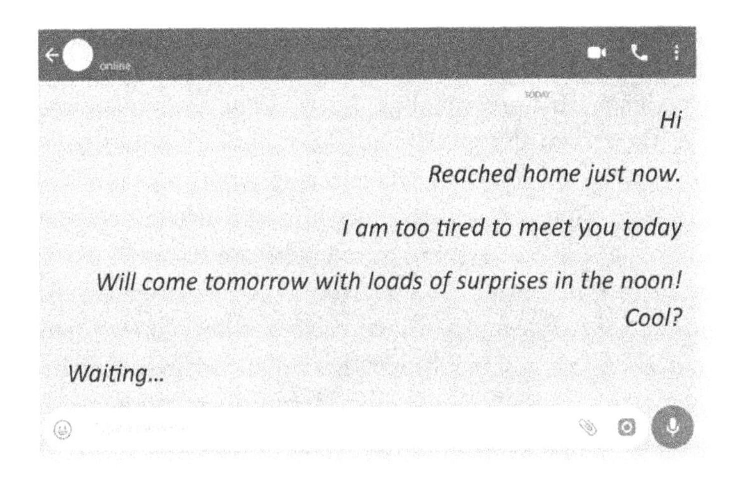

The shower of love of my mother contented my hurt heart that craved for love. After my divorce, I curbed my need to be loved. I choked up my feelings. I shared them with no one except Sameer. During all these years, I tried to stay away from India just to avoid bruising old wounds once again. However, it was Sameer that had brought me to India. He was now the pillar of my strength and one good reason to be happy in my life. I very well knew that one day he would find someone who would become his life. But that was fine. At least our friendship helped me in forgetting the associations I had with India and Rohan.

After I freshened up, I ate lots of food; after all, it had been a long time since I relished my mother's taste. More than the food, her love pacified me, and I slept all day long.

* * *

I was going to visit his home today. After I had got closer to Sameer, I had also got close to uncle and aunty too. We all shared a great connection by now. They loved me like their own daughter. They knew how we had been great supports for each other during our rough times.

I was super excited to meet him and them. I took a sling bag that Sameer had gifted me from his first salary, put the gifts inside and started walking towards his home. Like other girls loving their crushes, I never had to dress up when I met him. What an unfortunate person I was. The first man I loved had left me for another girl, and the second man, for whom I had fallen for, was gay. While thinking about all this, I never realised when I reached his home. Sameer's father opened the door with his cheerful smile.

"Hello, Preeti, how are you? We all are very happy that you are back. Welcome to India. I don't have to worry about Sameer because now you are here."

I touched his feet, and he patted on my head and gestured blessing me.

"Oh no, uncle, in fact now my mother feels that they would see me ever-smiling, for Sameer would always be there to cheer me up!" saying I took a seat on the couch. Sameer walked out of the kitchen with a tray full of delicious cuisines. "Surprise... surprise!! Here is something special for my dearest Preeti." I had never seen him so full of life and energy before. He had transformed into a young, enthusiastic man. I had seen him on video calls and on Facebook, but meeting face to face was really different. He was now a handsome young dashing man, very confident and well-groomed, as opposed to the vulnerable and naive schoolboy I had seen years back. I kept on looking at him, mesmerized.

As he gave me a tight hug, something moved in me with his touch. I felt a flutter inside me. I had to control myself. *'Stop falling for him. Don't forget that he is gay'*, I reminded myself, curbing my attraction at the spur of the moment.

His mother raced with kettle and cups, and I distracted myself by helping her place them on the table by rearranging other things.

"Sameer has made *Pav Bhaji* for you, and I have fried some *Pakoras*. Hope you like them. He knew how you craved Indian fast food for a long time," said aunty.

"That's so sweet of you all!" I politely replied.

Sameer's mom was a very poised and warm-hearted lady. I loved her for her demeanour and her hospitality. Sameer had inherited her virtues. For a moment, while looking at Sameer, I felt lost and then turned to the gifts that were going to make him even happier than he was now.

I unchained the bag and took out things one by one.

"Here are some surprises!" I said while taking out and handing over the neatly wrapped gifts. I had brought a professional camera for uncle, a food processor for aunty, and the newest iPhone for Sameer. Sameer was crazy for new phones. It was a surprise for him, and the moment he opened the gift wrap, I got the most cherishable expression from him for my lifetime.

"Preeti... he came close and gave me a playful punch on my cheek. How dare you bring such an expensive gift for me?" I smiled happily. I loved the way he behaved with me. I felt, even this was enough to spend my life alone. I felt like kissing him, but I distracted myself again. After I had developed feelings for him, his proximity sent a feeling of deep pain inside. I tried my level best to conceal my feelings. The fear of losing him as a friend was scarier than living life alone or even seeing him with another man.

After feasting on the cuisines, it was time to eat chocolates that I had brought from the US. I felt delighted to see him relish Lindt that he loved the most. We had a great time chitchatting together. When I said goodbye and got going, Sameer said he would walk with me to my place. I felt that deep yearning for while listening to Sameer. I felt like holding his hand that moment. But I controlled my emotions from flying high, and with a quick good night wave, I rushed home. As I peeped down through my window, I could see a smudged image of Sameer in the tears which trickled down my eyes.

37

The biggest shock

It was for the first time after so many years I had met Sameer. An evening with Sameer's family felt so special and refreshing. Today, here I was, sitting on the balcony with Sameer chitchatting like those olden days. This felt even more special. I could not believe that this was coming true. A coffee mug and French fries had spiced up our talks. We talked for hours together. Sameer narrated to me about his confrontation with his parents. He also told me how his father had been making efforts to befriend him. He told me about his dating experiences and promised me that he was never going to turn to the world that had no emotional gains. I felt very much at peace after hearing this from him.

From that day onwards, we started spending time with each other after returning from our office and enjoyed weekends together. We started shopping every Saturday and hanging out on streets. We also joined a gym. I had some weight reduction targets, so even he joined me in my daily morning jog. Life had taken a new leaf. As people in our society saw and learnt about us hanging out together, they started gossiping about us.

Somewhere it made me happy as our names were being taken together in gossips.

One day we returned from the gym, and I was making sandwiches for us. I kept on looking at him unknowingly, and he caught me.

He asked, "What are you thinking?"

"Sameer, sometimes I feel life doesn't give all that we deserve. I stay with my mom, but I share more with you. My brother doesn't speak to me, nor does his wife. Though my mother stays in this house, her emotions find their way to my brother and her grandson. I share everything with you, but you are gay. What sense does this make anyway?"

"Preeti, nothing is perfect. This is life. Let's be happy that at least your mother stays with you, and she loves you."

"Hmm..." I replied.

I wished he could understand how I wished we were a family. I was trying to tell him that I had started spending more time with him than my family. But how foolish I was to tell him all this. Even if he knew I loved him, it was never going to change the status of our relationship or his emotions or even his gender.

The doorbell rang, and my mother entered the house with bags full of vegetables and groceries. Her arrival interrupted our conversation.

"Hi aunty, how are you? Let me help you," saying that, dutiful Sameer ran to help my mother. After keeping the bags in the kitchen, he said, "Aunty, I will leave now, will see you later. Bye." He wore his footwear and quickly left with a cute wave for a goodbye.

After he left, my mother asked, "Preeti, people are talking about you and Sameer. Even some of our relatives have seen you both hang out together. They keep on taunting me about you being in a relationship with a boy so young."

"Oh mamma, please... I can't believe even you think we are together. We are friends, mother. Nothing is going on in between us," I answered.

"If you really love him, I don't mind you marrying him, dear. He is such a nice boy."

"No, mamma, nothing is going on between us!" I swallowed my feelings and tried to tell her the fact.

"Are you sure? I have never seen you so happy and passionate about your life. I see you smiling after a long time. That glow on your face speaks of the bliss in your life."

She was right. I was in love. But how could I tell her that?

"Are you sure you don't like him, or is it that he likes you?"

"Ma, alright, let me tell you the truth." I pulled her hand and made her sit on the bed.

I decided to tell her.

"Maa, he is gay. Please don't tell this to anyone, and that's why we both are like two male friends or two female friends, so there can be nothing in between us."

"I had never imagined that in my life. Oh, so you are a gay activist, and he is gay. Now I understand the common grounds of your friendship. But I had never imagined that someone as simple as Sameer can be gay."

"Even you are speaking like others, mom. Anyone can be gay. There is nothing to do with simplicity and character. He was born that way." I started telling her about his school days, his suffering, the rejections, and his loneliness. That day we chatted for a long time after a long.

The whole discussion drained the energy and positivity in me. How difficult it was for me to accept the fact myself. How I wished he would have been straight!

Later, my mother left to visit my brother's home. After my brother's marriage broke, our bond was broken as I stayed at my mother's place and some more financial matters. My mother had been busy with her grandson, and I encouraged it as it filled the vacuum in her life that developed due to my father's death.

I had also joined my new office and had I settled in my new world. After a month, my office shift changed, so our meetings had become very infrequent. One month passed. I was exploring my life on a fresh page. Happiness was in the air. I had a wonderful team under me, and I was enjoying the culture here.

* * *

One fine day, I returned from the office. The moment I stepped in, I was surprised to see him at my place at this time. He was sitting in my living room. Before I could ask him anything, he yelled, "Preeti, I have super news for you. I am so happy." I was confused; I was calm and composed usually and never got excited or terribly depressed.

"What is it, Sameer? You seem very excited!"

"Oh yes, I am. I am the happiest person on this Earth. Before I could listen to him, he gave me a tight hug. Abhijeet proposed to me. Do you remember him? We had once met him in the gym. Look, these are the flowers he gave me today!!"

"I am so happy, Preeti. You won't imagine... how my life has taken a turn!"

He had come out of the blue in Sameer's life. I was dumbstruck, and it was visible on my face. I tried my level best to hide my emotions and brought a fake smile on my face making an attempt to appear genuine.

"That's wonderful... I am so happy for you. You never told me about him. I will change and come, and then you tell me the entire story." The lost colour of my face did not escape his eyes.

He asked me, "Are you upset, Preeti?"

"Umm yes... I had an argument with my boss, and he said things to me. Chuck... let's talk," I lied.

This lie was convincing as he knew how touchy I could get when it comes to my work. To hide my face, I disappeared into my room. I rushed to the washroom and cried. I could not control my tears. I was getting so involved in him, and now his relationship status had also changed. This was bound to happen. I tried to console myself. I always wanted to see him happy. But this was not so easy now. I closed my eyes and determined to control the outburst of my feelings. I changed into a t-shirt and track pants, combed my hair, and came out with a cup of tea and biscuits. We sat at our regular place.

"How are you? You look very handsome in this yellow t-shirt that Preeti has gifted you," said my mother, who was in a great hurry.

"I'll see you later. I have cooked some *Aloo Tikkis* for you. Please help yourself," she added and left for her evening walk.

"So, tell me the story," I tried suppressing my sorrow and pain with a glass of water on the table. I had to take this with a pinch of salt. I tried my level best to act normal.

"I met Abhijeet a couple of months back. Do you remember that man who met us at Pheonix mall? That time he was just an acquaintance of mine." He went on with excitement.

He opened the gallery on his mobile and showed me a photo.

"He is from Mumbai," saying that, he held his phone in front of me.

It was a selfie of Abhijeet and Sameer. The moment my eyes fell on the picture, I sensed Sameer was kissing on his cheek, and their eyes shone with immense bliss. I envied that man.

"He had come to Pune for one of his company projects," said Sameer breaking the silence.

"Do you remember I told you last month that a stranger went out of the way to get me petrol in a bottle when my bike went dry? He was Abhijeet."

I wondered what was in that man he had fallen for. How come a man with such an average appearance had attracted Sameer? He wasn't even his type. I felt a pang of jealousy stinging me.

"That was the time I came to know he worked in a company which was on the same floor as mine. After that one incident, we started meeting at the smoking zone frequently during office break hours and became great friends. He is the first person in my life after you with whom my interests match so well."

Oh, so it was Abhijeet because of whom Sameer had started returning late from his office. He went on with the story, and I pretended that I was interested in listening.

"Though initially I never looked at him that way, but as we met more frequently, I fell in love. We became good friends. I had even told him I was gay as I found him very broadminded. Later we started meeting frequently in a small eatery nearby our office for lunch. We got closer that time. Abhijeet belongs to a very poor family. His dad passed away in his childhood. His mother is a primary teacher who brought him up with huge hardships."

Sameer spoke about him with such great emotional intensity that it was difficult for me to accept.

"But I had never imagined that he could be gay too. So, I had never let my crush grow. I was scared of another rejection. Even he had been acting like he was not gay. I can't believe he proposed to me today." saying he blushed.

"The sad part of the story is, his project is over, and he is going back." As he talked about their parting, his grief was clearly visible in his eyes.

"Preeti, speaking on a positive note, I am the luckiest man on this earth. We need two things to complete our life, one is a best friend, that is you, and the other is love that I have found in him. The best part is he wants to commit to me."

I felt happy that I was one part that completed his life.

"Oh, thank you, Sameer," I reacted with a mask on my face. Somewhere in my mind, I questioned myself. Why couldn't I control my feelings? It was too late for everything.

"Let's celebrate it then. Have you told your parents?" I said, trying to show I am really happy.

"Yes, I will, Preeti, but I wanted to tell you first, so I came to meet you here."

"That's so nice of you. I am so glad that you value me so much!" I exclaimed sincerely.

He kept on narrating the whole story of the whole one month for two long hours. Most of it slipped off my ears. I was unable to comprehend what he spoke as I was in a state of disappointment. My life and rejections from the days before my marriage kept flashing in front of my eyes. I felt guilty and sorry for him that I was not able to give my best as a friend. I felt it was my failure. In case of Rohan, I had proved to be the best friend and wife, but in this case, I could not understand why I was not able to digest the fact in the same way as before. Something in me had broken. I was not at all strong the way I was before. He left after two hours, and I spent a sleepless tearful night.

38
A dawn

When I was trapped in the dark dungeons of Tanmay's memories, I had no courage to face myself in the mirror. I hated myself for everything that I had done. Amidst the guilt and dilemma about dating, one incredible thing happened to me that gave me my lost 'self', that was Abhijeet.

Abhijeet Kumar was very different from other men I had met in my life. He was a simple man with a thin body structure and an average height of 5 feet 5 inches. This average looking witty man had an aura of purity. I had a thing for him. I loved listening to his baritone voice when he spoke. I had not seen but heard him for the first time.

It was noon, and I was already late for my office. I was tired of riding to my office in the scorching sun. I had forgotten to refill my petrol tank, so my bike stopped. I was caught in the middle of traffic. Irritated with the honking horns, I rushed to unblock the way for other vehicles on the road. With great effort, I dragged my bike to the roadside and parked it. While I was checking for petrol pumps on Google maps, a man called me out from a car parked behind me.

"Hey, do you need any help?" he asked. Even during that worrisome moment, his voice attracted me.

I indicated with my index finger pointing at the petrol tank of my bike and said, "No fuel!"

"I can arrange for some petrol for you if you want," he said. The signal went green, and this stranger vanished in the fleet of other cars before hearing a reply from me. I waited for fifteen minutes, and he came back. This man had managed to get some petrol for me in a bottle though it was illegal.

I felt highly obliged that he had gone out of the way to help me. I paid him for the petrol and thanked him. When I asked him where he works, I was happy to find out he happened to work in a company located on the same floor as mine. I wanted to reciprocate him in some way later, so I asked him for his mobile number. He took mine too.

"Good to know we are neighbours," he smiled.

"Let's meet up after the office once! I owe you a treat," I said, showing my gratitude.

"Done!!" he said with a 'thumbs-up'.

"I have to rush to the office. Ping me on WhatsApp. Catch up with you later. Bye," he smiled and went away.

I was impressed by his gesture. I wondered how come such people exist in this selfish world. I was genuinely impressed by him. Retrospectively I feel glad that I had forgotten to refill my bike. I wouldn't have met this helpful, honest, polite, responsible, and understanding man otherwise.

A couple of days passed, and I met him in the lift after my office was over.

"Hi," I said with astonishment, unexpectedly meeting him here.

He gave one of his best smiles and asked, "You owe me a treat for that day. Would you like to join me over a coffee?"

"Of course, let's go!" I said.

His one offer had opened the golden doors of my future. We had a small talk over a coffee and smoke and took no time to become good friends. We kept chatting, and I did not realise that it was almost an hour, though it felt like ten minutes. I was brought back to reality with Preeti's call.

"Hi, haven't you reached home?"

"Umm, no... I will be late today. Let's meet up later." I disconnected the call, continuing my chat with him. I did not tell Preeti about this immediately as I had never thought this man could be gay too. I knew my crush was not going to make sense anyway. I just wanted to be nice to him because he had been very helpful to me.

For the next two days, whenever I passed his office, my feet lingered, and my eyes searched him. I knew his shift timings and wished I could catch a quick glance at him. I yearned to meet him and kept wondering whether I should let it happen coincidently or take a direct initiative. Perhaps telepathy helped, and after a couple of days, he called me up. He asked me if I would join him for coffee again. After that, we started meeting frequently. No wonder I thought I could easily make friends with people, unlike my college days. Many of my colleagues and even strangers liked my company, so his interest in spending time raised no doubts about his intentions. I had easily learnt to remain in the closet, which helped me establish a decent network of friends and acquaintances.

I still remember the evening when I met him for the second time. It was one more co-incident. I had stepped out of my office when it rained cats and dogs. I was rushing to catch my company bus when suddenly someone pulled me from behind into a big black umbrella. When I turned around, I was astounded to find him.

I felt so romantic. By that time, I had developed a more intense feeling for him. Something felt similar to my past. The clouds thundered, it heavily rained, and a loving hand was around my shoulders. His hand slightly played with the hair near my neck as we walked under one umbrella.

"Come with me to the parking. I will drop you home. I have a spare raincoat in the dickey. Let's go!" saying that, he literally pulled me. A wave of heat emerged in the cool rains, making me feel even warmer. That was the time I suspected that even he was gay. The spark which I now felt lit between us was a proof of that.

As days passed, we started meeting more often. A different bond was being knitted in us, letting my feelings take some shape. We had now started meeting for lunch almost every day and even for evening tea. I wanted to tell Preeti about this. But with the background of Tanmay's rejection, I dare not share this with her. I feared she might discourage me and spoil my romanticism. So, I kept telling everyone I had certain targets and needed to stay back at my office for long.

This continued for almost twenty days, and one fine day he called me at 7 p.m. "Can you meet me after the office at the cafe. Let's have coffee before you leave. I have to go back to Mumbai soon. My project is over."

I missed my heartbeat for a moment. I felt a wave of depression enveloping me. I felt like his words were suffocating me. I was unable to breathe. I was going to miss him. Finally, it was his time to leave, weaning the blooming emotion in my heart. I was very nervous and anxious to meet him. I did not want to let him go. But I had to face this parting. It was my mistake to fall for someone who was never going to stay with me. I speeded towards the cafe. He was waiting with a bouquet in his hand.

"I had my farewell today," he said. I had understood that when I saw that bouquet in his hand. He told me about how happy he felt being here, how he would miss our time, and about his plans to revisit Pune. We spent around one hour chitchatting.

Though I tried to smile, the grief that I had been trying to suppress was constantly surfacing up.

"Will you drop me near your home today? I have some work in the city area. I have to shop something for my mom," he asked.

I felt better as I thought I was going to get some more time with him. I happily said yes, and we got going. After travelling some distance, we reached a low traffic place, and he said, "Sameer, could you please park the car at the side?"

I parked my car and kept on looking at him in confusion!

My heart started beating faster."

"Uhh... what happened?" I asked.

"Just a moment, please stop. I want to speak to you," he said.

"This is for you," he said, handing over the bouquet to me.

I was flabbergasted.

"Thanks," I said with a smile and blushed. His eyes were looking at me very intently, and I felt captivated.

"Sameer, I love you, and I know you have the same feelings for me too. Your face speaks more than your words, Sameer."

I could not believe it. Someone whom I liked and had slowly started feeling for, had the same feeling for me. His words contented my heart. I felt so blessed at that moment. I kept staring at him for a long time with my emotions overflowing from my eyes and my smile not ready to leave my face. He kept our office bags to cover the front glass and gave me a quick kiss on my lips.

The kiss conveyed the deep emotions he had for me. The signal behind us went green, and we could not hug. But now, our eyes said more than the words. I knew I had found the true love, my soulmate, my life!

* * *

He had left for Mumbai. I could still smell his perfume on my cheek and my shirt. My life had taken a turn from that day. I had opened up about us to Preeti and my parents too. My dad and mom were happy that I had found someone who was willing for a serious relationship. I had some hopes that I could settle down with him some day. He had liked Pune and had said that he might find a job here, and we could even stay together. I had started planning for our future together. I was even thinking of buying a flat for both of us.

Our long-distance relationship was a little easier due to endless hours of chat and a well-kept commitment to meet every weekend. Though his mother was sick, he kept his promises related to our dates. Him keeping his words touched me the most.

In a couple of months, a man who was a stranger had become my life. I spent five days of the week finishing my project and fled to Mumbai to spend weekends with him. We spent our nights going for long drives and other times in hotels. I was busy juggling with my work and Abhijeet's calls. My meetings and WhatsApps with Preeti had gradually decreased. But for true friends, time and distance made no difference, so I knew she would certainly understand me.

* * *

Irritated with the 'Monday blues' I was drinking green tea in my office cafeteria, all alone. . I had not got a single message from Abhijeet for a long time. I kept checking my phone every five minutes. I called him feeling worried and was shocked to hear his panicked voice.

"Sameer, come to Mumbai ASAP. My mother had a heart attack this morning, and she is in ICU. I will text you the address," he said.

I spoke to my boss, that there was a family emergency, informed my parents and left for Mumbai by my car. I reached the hospital in not more than three hours.

* * *

When I reached the fourth floor of the hospital, I saw Abhijeet sitting on a bench. His face showed some relief.

"Hi Abhi, how is aunty now?"

Abhijeet looked quite alright, and he smiled. "Doctor said things are very much under control, and she would be fine soon. I brought her here in the nick of time. Things would have been worst otherwise."

Abhijeet did not allow me to go inside; I wondered why. When I kept asking him, he got restless. He did not speak much. Looking at him, I realised he must have been hungry for a long, so I got some sandwiches for him from the cafeteria.

"Abhi, let me go and see her once, till then you finish the sandwiches," I pleaded.

"No, please don't. She will never want to see your face," he said hopelessly. "It's all my mistake." His eyes got wet.

I was baffled by this reaction of his. He had called me to Mumbai, and he said I shouldn't go and meet her. What had he told her about me? I wondered.

"I told her, Sam," he said with exasperation.

"One day, she told me that she wants to see me with someone now... someone who would love and care for me. I told her that I already have someone in my life. She was pleased and said she will accept anyone whom I love. I got carried away for that moment. As your parents had accepted our relationship, I somewhere felt I should give it a try. I confessed about us," he started weeping.

I was shocked to hear his thoughtless behaviour. I had warned him not to ever tell this to his mother. We had decided to keep it a secret.

"How foolish of me that I told her. It's my mistake.", and silent tears rolled down his cheek as he spoke.

"What happened after that?" I probed further, biting my nails.

"You know, how short-tempered she is. She got furious. She said I will have to walk over her dead body. She was not at all ready to accept that I am gay. She said this is a curse of God or something. She blamed me, and she blamed you for changing my orientation. She said that she will never see your face again. She kept on warning me that if I stay in a relationship with you, she will kill herself. I fought with her," continued Abhijeet.

It was really stupid of him to blurt this out. This silly mistake of his had made a big mess.

"She was furious and made me promise that I would never stay with you. She even blackmailed me that if I don't listen to her, she will commit suicide. None of us spoke to each other for a week. Today when she was having a bath, she had a heart attack. I called the ambulance, and we rushed to the hospital."

"Two hours before you came, she gained consciousness. When I met her that time, you know what she said, *'Promise me, son, you will not do that sin again, or else you will see me here one more time and probably the last time.'* "

"I will never be able to stay with you. You may call me spineless or whatever. Sorry, Sameer, we can't be together anymore. I will meet you occasionally but as friends. I will never be able to continue with the relationship. I know how much pain I have given to my mother. I can never hurt her again. When my father passed away, she started taking tuitions of school students, provided lunch services, and withstood the financial burden all alone. She has made countless sacrifices for me. You have no idea how much suffering she has undergone throughout her life. I don't want to be the cause of more," he was almost in tears as he said this.

I could not say anything after this. His avalanche of emotions for his mother froze my words. I knew how much he loved his mother, and I had a premonition that she will never accept me the way my parents had accepted him. I had nothing to say but to accept that it was all over.

I was totally numb after hearing this. I tried to check my phone to distract myself. Abhijeet always kept promises and commitments. But perhaps he had forgotten that he had promised something to me too. But the mama's boy had forgotten it and had chosen his mother over me. I felt dejected.

I tried to divert my mind and checked my phone.

I was surprised to find *10 missed calls and 50 WhatsApps* of Preeti. She never contacted me desperately unless there was a reason.

I wondered why Preeti had been trying to call me. So, I opened her chat.

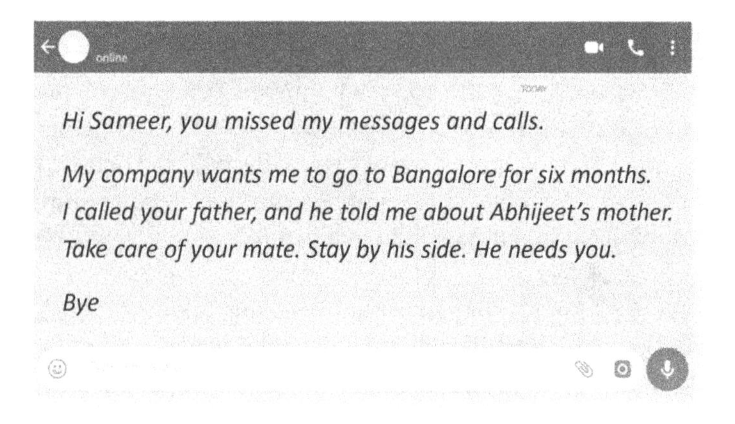

Too many things were happening all at the same time. I felt really stressed. I was shattered. Our weekend meetings were going to stop forever. My love story had met a dead end. I remembered the astrologer's words. I was going to stay single forever. When

I needed Preeti by my side, she was leaving the city. I felt deeply saddened.

While I was lost in my thoughts, a nurse came running out of the ICU, "Mr Abhijeet? Please come inside."

After went in and when he came out, he said that his mother is better. His face beamed with a smile. He said that I should go back by tomorrow. But I convinced him that love goes beyond everything and he should allow me to stay as I was his true friend too. His mother did not know me, so I convinced him to tell her I am a colleague of his and stayed there for some days. It was my duty to be with him when he needed me. He had no close relatives except one lady in the neighbourhood who helped them.

It was the first and last time we were going to spend time together. We were not going to meet each other unless needed, and our communication was also going to be restricted. True love was a sacrifice, he had done for his mother, and I had to do the same to respect his emotions.

39

A dead end

I had done all that I could do. I helped Abhijeet in every possible way and came back to Pune. When my parents heard about the line separating us, they were deeply saddened. All they could do was empathize with me. They knew my life was going to test my strength and patience in every possible way. They felt very concerned about me. Preeti was now in Bangalore, and Abhi and I had broken up.

I had just begun living a golden page in my life, and this unexpected breakup had cropped up out of the blue.

One day I was sitting in the living room, feeling frustrated and hopeless. My mother patted lovingly on my shoulders, "Why don't you call Preeti? Tell her what is troubling you. You will feel better. It has really been long, and you haven't been in touch with her," said my understanding mother.

She was right. I had not been in touch with Preeti. The reason was her change in behaviour that was constantly annoying me. It was neither her mistake nor mine. I had suddenly isolated myself from everyone after I had got closer to Abhijeet. I guessed it. I had hurt her. Maybe

I had taken her for granted. If not Preeti, from whom could I expect this level of understanding?

So not letting the ego spoil our relationship further, I called Preeti.

"Hi Preeti, how are you? I am back in Pune. Sorry I could not receive your calls at that time. I was in the hospital with Abhijeet," I explained.

She said nothing except *'I am fine'*, which also did not sound true.

"When did this project come up, Preeti? You never told me you had plans to go to Bangalore?" I asked.

There was a long pause. "Did you ever remember I existed?" her voice sounded choked. I could hear her sob.

"Did you ever tell me you went to Mumbai? I came to know that from your parents," she sounded very hurt.

"Anyway, tell me, how is Abhijeet's mother?" she asked formally.

Somewhere I felt it did not really matter to her.

"She is fine," I replied.

"How is Abhijeet now?" she asked.

"He is fine too. But tell me, Preeti, you must have known about your project at least a month before. Why didn't you tell me before I went to Mumbai?" I asked.

"Did you ever text me after you guys started dating? You enjoyed your weekends with him. You had no time for me," she shouted angrily.

"I thought you would understand. My time was his right, Preeti. He loved me, and he was my boyfriend," I justified.

"So being in a relationship gave you all rights to turn down your closest friends. Didn't it?" she taunted.

Perhaps she had not noticed the word 'was' in my sentence.

"No... I don't mean that. I just thought you would understand," I said.

I tried my best to tell her my side, but she ignored my justifications.

"Look, Sameer, you cannot take me for granted," said Preeti.

She was impatient now, and she seemed badly hurt. She had started fighting with me, and that was unusual.

"I am sorry, Preeti. I hurt you. I took you for granted. My bad! Please forgive me," I pleaded.

There was yet another long pause. She wept and sniffed her nose while gathering her words.

"But please don't do this to me ever again," she said.

"Alright, I promise," I tried to assure her.

"How long are you going to stay there?" I asked.

"It's going to be for another six months or more. How does that matter to you now? You enjoy your life with Abhijeet," she taunted.

"It's not the way you think. We are not together anymore," I said.

"What are you saying? When did this happen?" her sarcastic tone showed some genuine concern now.

"I am sorry. I did not know about it," she said, sounding softer and more understanding now.

I started the story and poured my heart out. I felt better.

"I am so sorry, Sameer. I did not know about this. Please forgive me. Sorry for being sarcastic. I really did not know about your breakup," she confided genuinely.

There was a long pause.

"You can talk to me any time you feel like. Take care," she said and quickly disconnected the call. This was so unlikely of her.

After speaking to her, I could not sleep the entire night. I kept on mulling over why she had an initial emotional outbreak. Plus, I could note a trace of relief when she expressed her concern for me. This was very much unexpected. Maybe she felt it because she sought emotional support from me. Whatever the situation was, I had to find it out.

40

Moving on

A month had passed after our break-up, and I had already accepted that life will always be unfair to me. There wasn't a moment that we did not text each other, but now I wasn't allowed to call him for days. It could be any time of the day; every little thing reminded me of Abhijeet. It could be my changed disciplined routine or my changed preferences for food. It could be his favourite t-shirt, colour around or a song on FM. If I switched on the television, his favourite movie reminded me of him, or if I simply went to the kitchen, even the aroma of coffee was enough to trigger a series of memories with him. He was anywhere and everywhere in my mind.

I did not feel like going back to the office. The places where we hung out, the restaurants where we ate, constantly reminded me of him. I felt as if Pune was eating me up. Even when I stepped out of my office, my eyes lingered over the entrance of his office. It was going to be very difficult. My whole life was going to be so full of him. His thoughts stirred my soul all the time.

I was sitting on my bed with a sullen face, and my parents pushed the door open. "It has been a long time

Sameer. We know what you must have gone through. Life is getting complicated for you. See, let a few days pass, and we will invite Abhijeet to our place and have a word with him. Maybe I can convince him to get back with you," said my father, keeping his hand around my shoulder and sitting beside me.

I looked at my father, my eyes met his, and I smiled. I felt fortunate to have a father like him. He was so supportive after I had kept my promise and found that one man for my life.

"Thanks, Dad. I am so lucky to have you," I said and gave him a warm hug.

My mother sat on my other side and said, "It's Monday tomorrow. Go to your office and start your life on a fresh page. Let us try to speak to Abhijeet and see what he has to say. I am also thinking to speak with his mother if he gets convinced. Maybe, a mother to mother talk can change her perspective,".

So, I built my hopes on the trust in my parents' convincing power and reassured myself that it was just a matter of time and one day there would be dawn in my love life too.

41

Throwing away the mask

I had accepted that my life was going to test the limit of my patience. I had decided to wait. One thing kept on bothering my mind constantly. The failure in my love was only because I was gay. Had Abhijeet not revealed about it, we would be going steady today. What if being gay had not been taboo? What if people were more broadminded? What if Abhijeet's mother was like mine? In that case, at least Abhijeet wouldn't have distanced me like this.

It was very important for people to accept the fact that being gay was as natural as being a man or woman. A man marrying a man was as natural as a man marrying a woman. But more awareness was needed for this to happen. More gays were needed to come out of the closet to make this dream a reality.

I then remembered my mother saying a couple of months back, '*Sameer, my friends keep on asking me whether you are looking out for girls to get married, what should I tell them?*'

I had told my mom, '*Tell them, mom, I will marry late.*'

She was not convinced by this. She had asked me further, '*Son, I can shut their mouths now, but what do I do later? One day they will come to know when you and Abhijeet...*'

Abhijeet was no longer my boyfriend. But one thing was for sure, people were surely going to question me about it one day or the other. That night I kept thinking about what I should do. Something in me had changed. If I didn't respect my orientation, how will people respect mine? If I don't respect my sexual orientation, how will Abhijeet's mother respect it? If I have to pull him out of the guilt, the only way to do it was to start with me. If I don't come out of the closet, how would many others like me dare to? If more people come out of the closet, the increasing number will make it easier to prove the naturalness of being gay. It would be then people would slowly and steadily accept our community. So, I decided to make my gender public.

That night I posted on social media.

> "Hello, all!
>
> Before you judge me, let me tell you I am a human being and, yes, a good human being. My sex is male, but my gender is not. I am physically a man, but when it comes to my emotions, I am not like most other men. So, I am a cis-man. Yes, I am gay, and I am proud to be gay. I respect my gender. Will you respect mine?"

This post spread like wildfire. It became viral with thousands of comments, likes; some expected, some unexpected; some progressive remarks, some regressive.

I had done this without informing my parents. But I had enough strength to face the world with my true image. I looked into the mirror on the wall and smiled.

Today the old Sameer had vanished. I saw a new Sameer in the mirror, someone who has a purpose in life. Someone who has accepted himself and the situations around, the way they were. Today I stood to face the world with my true identity. I had to preserve this strength as I was going to face the unexpected and painful effect of my boldness. Not just me, but my family too. The next morning was perhaps the most difficult one for me and my family. The real challenge was to face the people, and I was ready for it.

* * *

After a sleepless night, constant vibrations of my mobile phone opened my eyes. With sleepy eyes, I checked my phone. I had many WhatsApps, some from my friends appreciating my courage while others said they never ever thought about it. I checked my Facebook and saw the notification icon red with a fat number, and closed my phone. As I was in an MNC that supported the LGBTQ community, I had nothing to worry about on that front.

When I went to the living room in the morning, I saw my mother and father checking Facebook and replying to texts. They appeared stressed and were frowning. My mother saw me coming out.

She looked at me, burst out with irritation, "What is going on, son? I am getting calls from my close friends, and so is your father. You should have informed us before letting this out. This is very painful and upsetting. I don't know how am I going to face this," she was very disturbed.

"Sorry, mom, for doing this impulsively. But I did it before I could change my mind," I said.

My father was typing something on his phone, and he looked at me and said, "I am tired of replying and receiving phones. I am not talking to anyone anymore. I was anyway prepared to face it when I had said you can shift to Mumbai. But this social media post of you has created a blast. You should have at least given us some idea so we would have been ready to face it."

"Hmm," I replied sadly.

He turned towards my mother, "Stop replying and responding to these calls, Mina. Just relax... our first priority is our son and not society. It's going to be very difficult, I know, but it totally depends on our attitude as to how we take it."

Look what my brother Vineet has messaged me,

'It is a blemish on our family that your son has shamelessly declared that he is gay. I abhor the way you have brought him up and what character he has developed. We would be ashamed to accept or even tell people he is our relative. As an elder brother, you should have discussed this with me.' my father read out and exhaled heavily.

"Anyway, Sushant, that man needs a reason to criticize us all the time. How can your sibling behave this way? A few years back, they used me, and now it's Sameer," said my mother vehemently.

Avoiding answering my mother, he steered the conversation to the original topic.

"This is now going to spread like wildfire. Your uncles and aunties are finding this difficult to accept. Look at their WhatsApps," said my father with a grim face.

"Dad, but at least my cousins have liked the post," I said.

"Sushant, your sister is calling me. How should I answer her? She must have played the card against me."

"Stop it, Mina, let's think about our son. I understand your issues with your in-laws, but this isn't the time to discuss" snapped my father.

My paternal aunt was now trying to bring this against my mother, blaming her for a bad upbringing. I had not thought how this post of mine would have a ripple effect on family politics.

My dad's face was crestfallen. Hiding the humiliation, he said, "Anyway, had Abhi and Sameer would have started living in, people would have questioned us one day. The earlier, the better!"

I heaved a sigh of relief. I was happy that my father had not scolded me for this, and he was supporting me.

"We don't care about anyone, Sameer. Your happiness is more important to us."

"Mom, dad, I feel very guilty about all that you both would have to face.

My phone rang, it was Preeti, "Sameer, you have finally done it! I truly appreciate your courage. It's going to be a tough time now, but the pleasure of liberation is far more precious. All the best, to you..." and we went on. I felt better that after a long time, we had an argument-less conversation. While I spoke to her, I could see my parents proudly smiling at me.

42

Together again

Though I had thought my relationship with Abhijeet would come to a dead-end, it did not. Although we had restricted our relation to certain limits, I had a hope that the guilt on his mind one day would find a way, and he would come back to me. After my parents took an initiative to convince Abhijeet, the flickering hope had brought some illumination in my life. I had started living life again. So, on this positive note, I said yes to the meet-up with my old friends. Finally, it worked out for all of us, and we all planned to meet in Goa.

All of us met at 'Lee Meridian'. Akash's boyfriend Harry had a membership there, and so we could get a discounted vacation at such a luxurious place. It was so good to see all of us together again. We had not met in years, except on video calls and group chats. It was a dream coming true and after a prolonged wait of years. It was such a pleasant thing to see ourselves; we all were chilling out at Miramar beach in Goa.

Each one of us had travelled a different path in life. All these paths led in different directions and had reached destinations far from one another. But at the bottom of our hearts, we were still those four schoolboys like old times. Akash and his boyfriend had settled in the US and started a startup in the area of energy management. They had started a family with two Persian cats and one pug. Vivek and Pranit were still single. Vivek was a company secretary, and Pranit looked after his family business.

We had not yet spoken our hearts out. But after we finished one kingfisher each, we all felt like those childhood days were back.

Akash began to speak,

"It feels so wonderful to be together again! Thanks, Sameer, it was all because of your insistence. So, what's up in your life?"

"Loads Akash! After I revealed my gender and my story about Tanmay, Dad has really become a buddy now. That's the only good part."

I took a deep breath and continued, "Like I told you guys on WhatsApp, Abhijeet and I aren't together anymore. Long story... forget it... life has been so unfair... even Preeti relocated to Bangalore. I feel so lonely."

So, I narrated things one by one. I told them about our friendship. I told them about Abhijeet. Then I narrated how our love changed the picture of my friendship and finally about my break-up with Abhijeet.

"Your story is painful indeed. You could have told this to us long back. You would have felt better. Why do you keep things to yourself?" said Pranit.

"But do you know what is the best part of this idiot's life?" asked Vivek.

"This man has someone who truly loves him despite a breakup, and he is damn lucky to have a friend like Preeti... and such supportive parents!" Vivek continued.

Looking at the sand beneath, I smiled sadly and took another drag of smoke.

"Pranit, one of our classmates had been spreading rumours about you that you are getting married to someone and then getting divorced," I asked, diverting the discussion from me to Pranit.

Pranit nervously avoided our eyes. He seemed anxious.

"Why are you silent, Pranit?" Akash asked

"Guys, this was not a rumour."

"What?" we all yelled in shock.

"I was forced to marry a girl. You know how my family is. Everyone gets married early. The day I joined my family business, they started looking for a girl even though I resisted a lot. Going against my father is impossible, you know that well. I dare not tell this to anyone. I married, and on the first night itself, she understood it, and I confided and apologized. The girl is a great soul. She did not use the law against me or my family. After we divorced, I helped her patch up with her ex-boyfriend and tried to resettle her. I convinced his parents to get them married. They will get engaged this year," said Pranit.

"It was good that you could settle her in her life. How unfair it was! How could you let this happen?" Vivek asked.

"After that incident, my parents have almost disowned me. We are not like you, Sameer. It is difficult when we have to face the opposition in the family itself. Overcoming it and moving ahead is in no way easy. But now, they had to accept it, though with reluctance. But since they are retired people and are dependent on me, they at least talk to me when they need anything," and he went on with his tale of woe.

There was a weird feeling in our minds. We all felt it. It seemed that the distance had separated us emotionally. Even our conversations sounded a bit artificial and unnatural.

"Don't you think the family system in India doesn't let you choose the lifestyle that you want? Why is it essential to stay with someone who is our partner? Why can't two people with no sexual interest stay together?" said Vivek.

I said, "What if we don't find anyone in our lives, Vivek and Pranit? We can stay together in our later life as friends instead of being all alone and lonely! What do you think? Pranit, you will always stay in Pune due to your family business. Vivek, you can come back to Pune after some years. Anyways your family will never move with you to Mumbai or even with your brother to Delhi. So how is the plan?"

All three of us gave a spontaneous hi-five!

The Goa air washed all our pains and complaints about our life. The waves of the sea dashed against the rocks and the shore and receded. Just like these, the waves of time carried the traces of sorrow in my mind, and the sultry breeze brought back my lost energy and freshness.

43

Mending the mistakes

After spending four relaxing days in Goa, I was waiting at Goa airport for my flight to Pune. I had checked in my luggage and wanted to kill time. I wished I could call Abhi, but he allowed me to call him once a week and text him once a day only. I texted Preeti when I found her online at this hour of dawn. She was very particular about her sleep routines. She never stayed awake at night unless something upset her. I assumed she must be very disturbed as she was online at this odd hour.

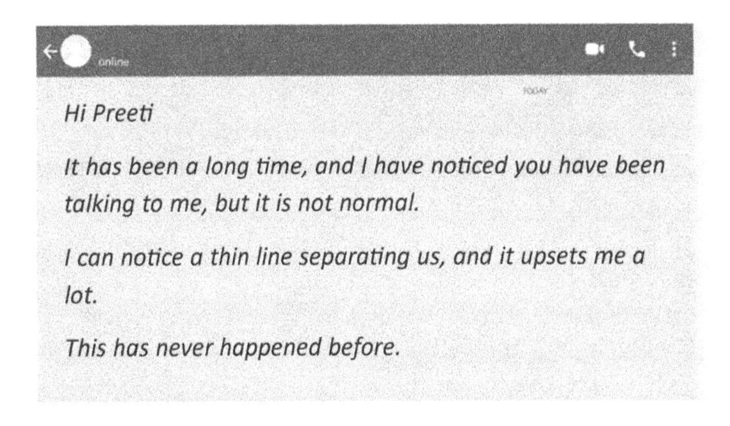

It was only after I got committed to Abhi. I might have taken you for granted or even hurt you, but my life has been a roller coaster since then.

Please forgive me, Preeti, and talk to me once the way we used to.

Two blue ticks, she had seen my message. After a couple of minutes, my mobile vibrated. It was Preeti calling.

"Hi, tell me Sameer, how are you?" she sounded very casual.

"I am not fine because I see that you are not fine," I said.

"When did that start affecting you?" she asked sarcastically.

I did not know how to react to this.

"Did it start from the day you came to know that your boyfriend will not stay with you? How could you take me for granted? I am not your mother to be available for you whenever you need me. I am your friend, so treat me like one," she bluntly said. She was never rude usually.

I kept on listening to her as perhaps I deserved that every word.

"Even I have some expectations from you. If you can't meet mine, don't expect anything from me. I am not going to tell you if something is wrong with my life," she curtly stated.

"If you cannot be there for me, why should I be dependent on you? Remember, every time you ask, my answer to you would always be *'I am fine,'* " she firmly said.

"Preeti... look," I tried to speak.

"It was I who called you every time, from when you posted on Facebook about your status, to when you felt low or even when you planned to go to Goa," she continued neglecting me.

"Do you ever remember calling me after you broke up with Abhi?" she asked.

"Sorry, Preeti, give me one last chance. Why do you speak so sarcastically nowadays? Please, forgive me once, my dear friend," I pleaded.

My apology calmed her for a moment.

She took a deep breath and said, "Okay," with a huge sigh.

I tried to switch the topic.

"Do you know all of my friends were asking about you?" I tried to butter her.

But she did not budge.

"Do you know what have we planned?" I changed the topic.

"Except for Akash, we all have decided to spend our life together if we don't find anyone in our life," I told her.

"Even I would join you then," she said.

Her reaction surprised me.

"If I don't find anyone even, I will come and stay with you that time. Is that fine?" she asked.

"Are you nuts?" I asked.

"That's because I am not going to marry anyone in my life. I am done for once. I would like to enjoy life with you gay guys instead," said Preeti.

"This is ridiculous!" I exclaimed. "Will you be comfortable to stay with men?" I asked.

"How does that matter when all of you are gays? It's almost like living with girls. People do this in the US. It's difficult in India, but maybe at some later point of time, it will become common," said Preeti.

"Lol... you have weird ideas Preeti, people will boycott us. They will not know whether we are bisexuals or gays. The society will point fingers at you," I said.

"Ah, I know! I was just kidding," said Preeti.

The talks went on and on after months together, and I felt better. My heart felt lighter. I wanted her to open up. I wanted her to heal. But something inside her had changed. She held a grudge, and it wasn't easy to cross the distance between us and reach her heart. I heard the announcement of the flight, and it was time for me to board. I disconnected the call and rushed with a quick goodbye. I promised to call her once I am back.

44

A ray of hope

The air in Pune felt dry after getting drenched in the intoxicating humid wetness of Goa. My dad had picked me up at the airport, and we were driving back home. It was after a long time that we had got some quality time together.

"How was your vacation, son?"

"Wonderful dad, it was after such a long time I enjoyed some quality time with my friends."

"Sameer, what is the status of your relationship now? Any progress?"

"Restricted, limited, and stagnant!" I said with a forced smile.

"Isn't there a way out that you and Abhijeet can stay together?" my dad spoke with deep concern.

"No, dad," I sadly replied.

"But have you thought about your future? What will you do if we are no longer there?"

"Dad, I have an answer for you now. I, Pranit and Vivek, have decided to stay together if we don't find a match," and thought my father might be pleased to know.

"Son, you say you would stay with your friends, but there is no form of commitment there. What if they find someone? What if you part your ways?" asked my father.

"My extension is over, and I am over 60. I am a heart patient too."

He asked with hesitation, "How about having a lesbian partner? You both can live your lives with mutual understanding and yet have stability."

"Dad, I don't want to do a marriage of convenience with a lesbian," I offensively reacted.

"I don't mean you should stay with a girl in specific. I just want you to find a partner for yourself. Marriage is not all about sex, though society feels so. It is about sharing things, my son. It's about a chat over breakfast. It's about solving the problems in life together. It's about complementing your weak areas with your partner's strengths. It's about care, and it's about your support. It's about planning for each other's future. It's about standing by each other during the worst," he said.

"Even Preeti married someone who was a perfect partner and trustworthy man, her best friend, but he cheated on her," I said.

"Sometimes, the lock of the marriage doesn't test true love. A true relationship stays even if there is no legal tie-up. It flourishes in freedom, and it nourishes with trust. The problem with the traditional marriage system is that it gives you no opportunity to test your love and locks you forever together. People break the rules only if they are laid. Love should be free with no rules and restrictions."

"But dad, there was enough space in their relationship."

"I don't know what Preeti has told you, but from what I know, it was more initiated by their family. I doubt whether Rohan had a choice. What your mother told me was, Rohan had a girlfriend, and Preeti was his rebound," said my father.

"I know that very well. Even Preeti has told me about it," I said.

"Hmm. Don't switch the topic of the conversation. What about you? How are you going to start a family?" asked my dad.

"Dad, I am gay. How can a family make any sense to me? Are you making fun of me? I can't produce kids with any lesbian or straight girl dad. I am very clear with it. I have seen what my friend has done," I firmly said.

"When did I ask you to produce kids?" A family not necessarily mean all that. Like you told me, even Akash and his boyfriend have started a family with pets. A family means a stable unit of people living together for a long period. If you and Abhijeet had settled down, I would have been the happiest father," he said.

"Dad, Abhijeet will never break the promise he gave to his mother," I said.

"Had you been my daughter and have broken up, I would have got you married to someone in an arranged marriage. Now listen, it's okay that you like men. How about registering on an LGBTQ matrimonial? Son, please think, what if your other friends, with whom you plan to stay, find mates? Commitment is easier between two people," he said.

"Dad, I don't trust the arranged marriages, irrespective of my orientation. Why can't I stay single? I have had enough in my life," I defended.

"Had you been a very strong man who is practical about life, I would have never felt so worried about you. You have always needed someone to share your emotions."

"I will manage it, dad, and Preeti will always be there," I replied.

"She isn't going to stay or spend her life with you. What if she might not be available when you need her? A friend cannot take the place of a life partner," he said.

"We will manage, dad. We go out of the way to help each other," I defended.

"Sameer, you don't have a sibling, don't forget that. You give me an option, and I will accept it," said he.

There was a long silence. After some time, something struck him suddenly, and he said, "Like we had previously thought, why not invite Abhijeet to our place. Tell him that we wanted to meet him once. It doesn't matter what relationship you guys have," he said.

"Alright, Dad, I will call him and invite him to Pune next weekend," I said.

I had a ray of hope now that this plan might change the whole picture. And yes, it really did.

45

Tough times

Sameer found Abhijeet, and my life one more time, was full of loneliness. I missed Sameer every weekend. In the beginning of the relationship, Sameer kept on giving me a few updates. But later, especially after their commitment, he gradually stopped. He was totally into Abhijeet, and his meetings with me got even more infrequent. He got so busy that it was always I who called him up or texted to ask how he was. I could not live with this vacuum. I wanted to run away from Sameer.

I saw a ray of hope when I got to know about an opportunity in Bangalore. As it was at a very short notice, most of my colleagues were reluctant to go. I thought this could be my best escape plan, so I said 'yes'. My cousin sister stayed in Bangalore, so shifting and settling down in the city was a cakewalk. So, I decided to go for a much-needed break in our friendship and embraced this opportunity.

When I went to Bangalore, I started breathing again. It was then, I was able to overcome my emotions I had for him. He had broken up with Abhijeet and now he needed me to fill the vacuum. He began his repeated attempts to talk to me. While I was thinking about this, my mobile buzzed. It was Sameer's WhatsApp. Think of the devil, and the devil is here.

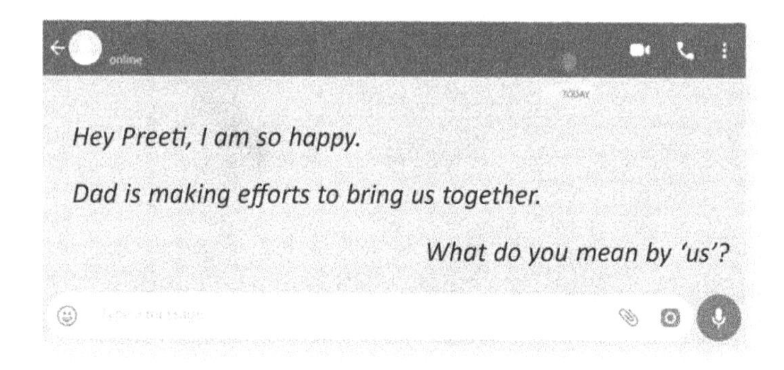

I missed a heartbeat for a moment!

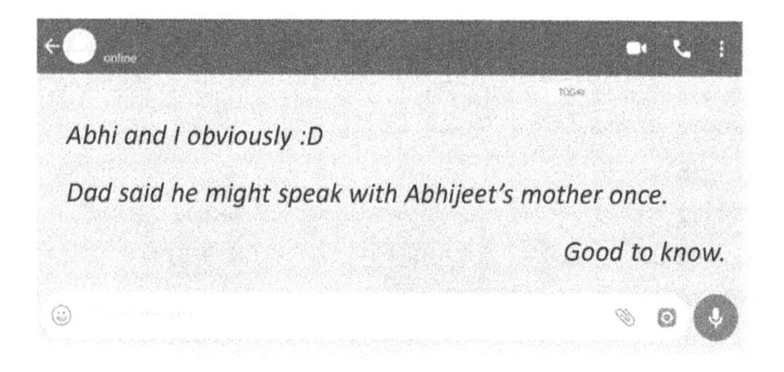

For a moment why I don't know, but I thought the word 'us' meant we both.

I texted formally. I wished it could have been us, but it was impossible to make him mine in this birth.

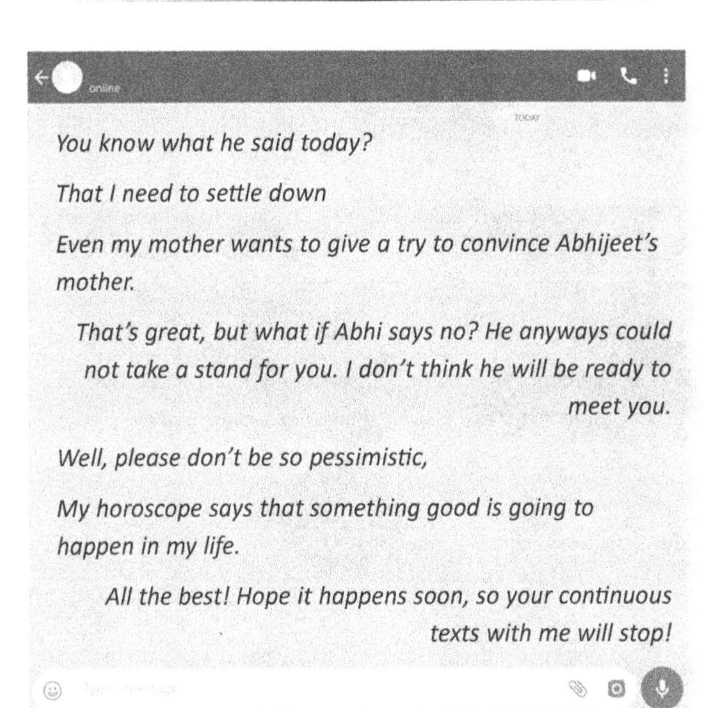

I had become so cynical these days.

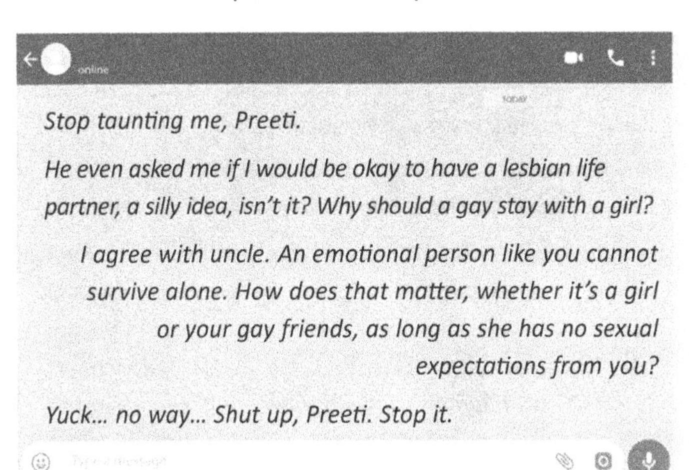

It was so suffocating. The father of my gay friend was asking him to stay with a girl. I simply could not imagine Sameer staying with another girl.

Preeti... how can you get serious about this fact. I told you what my father said and not what I want.

This is the problem with you Sameer, why do you bring up a topic if you are not interested in it and then change it when you want.

Why are you overreacting for no reason, Preeti?

A human is a social animal, and he or she needs someone to share his or her life with.

I disagree with you, Preeti. What about sexual needs?

You can meet them with your boyfriends.

You feel like sharing life with your sexual partner, not others. Alright, tell me, would you have been okay with such an arrangement?

Why not? There is nothing wrong. True love goes beyond all sexual needs. After a particular age, it's the companionship that matters and not those needs.

When Rohan fell for someone else, that did not stop me from loving him. Tell me one thing, the whole day, you chat with me like the way a boy chats with his girlfriend. You are so attached to me, and so am I. You seek support in me like your parents, and at times, I confide my sorrows in you like a child. Love doesn't have boundaries

Hmm.

Then tell me why do you stay with your parents?

Agreed! You have a point, Preeti.

Look, what matters is love and not orientation, to be a family. So, there is nothing wrong with thinking that way. If a girl doesn't mind you dating men, why should you mind staying with her? Though it would be painful sometimes, won't it be better than living without you?

I bit my lip. I made such a big blunder. Why did I blurt out my feelings? While talking about a hypothetical girl, I did not realise when I brought myself into the picture.

Love goes beyond desires. Do you think married couples feel attracted to each other all the time?

No, they don't, but still, they stay together. Why? People have affairs, but why do they continue with their marriages? One of the reasons is they need stability and care.

So, I feel such an unconventional relationship would certainly be better than a marriage in which you get cheated. It is better than marrying someone and losing the charm in the marriage. At least such an arrangement can guarantee freedom and can keep the love intact.

Frankly speaking, if I am asked to stay with someone like you, my life will get easier. I would get rid of your frequent texts and have a good room partner.

Stop kidding, Preeti. For a moment, I thought you were speaking about you and me.

:D :D

I concealed my feelings with a smile.

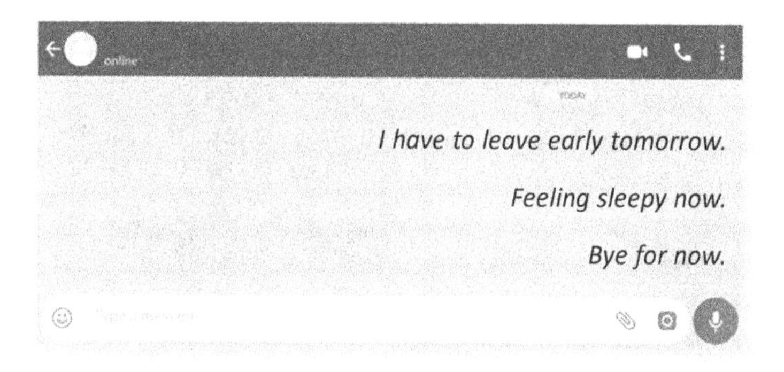

This conversation made me feel sick. How difficult it was for me to imagine myself at the place of such a girl! I wish this really happened to me. The whole night I kept thinking about it and had weird dreams about our life together.

46

The last unforeseen

I texted Abhijeet,

Drop me a line when you are free

It's something urgent and important.

Since last week, except for forwards and important things, he had restricted me from texting and calling. I was glad that he hadn't blocked me. It was also decided that this frequency was going to reduce. It was his way to get out of it. It gave me immense pain, but I was absolutely helpless.

After an hour, my WhatsApp said, Abhi is typing...

You can call me now.

I dialled his number.

I felt my voice choking, but I gathered the courage to speak after I heard his hello.

"Hi Abhi, how are you? How is your mom?" I asked out of concern.

"I am much better. We both are slowly getting over with our conflicts related to you," he said.

"What are you doing this weekend?" I asked.

"No plans as of now," he calmly replied.

"My parents want to meet you once in their life. Will you come to Pune?" I nervously asked.

"But Sam, we had decided that we are never going to meet each other. If you are trying to find reasons, it's a big NO, Sam," he said firmly.

"No, Abhi, I have told my parents that I will stay single forever. So, they wanted to meet that one and only man without whom my life is so incomplete.

"Hmm. Sameer, but we have decided we will never meet again. Things are not easy for me too. I remember our every single date and our pillow time when we used to have staycations on weekends. It haunts me day and night. But I can't go against my mother's wish. Had I not ever revealed the fact that I am gay, and I love you, I wouldn't have hurt her. Trust me, even I am never going to have anyone in my life. You would be the first and the last person with whom I fell in love."

"But no, Sameer, I will not meet you."

"But... my father..." I tried to speak, but he disconnected.

I felt frustrated and lost all hopes. But to my surprise, he called me back.

"Sorry for my reaction, but I thought I would get carried away. Yes, I will respect your father's wish and come to Pune. But please don't cross the line. Let's be friends and that too at a distance. We are not meeting after this visit," he said.

"Okay," I replied in disappointment.

I knew it was not going to happen. I had a premonition that it would be the last time we were going to meet. But what if my father convinces him and brings us together again? Would his mother get ready to have a word with mine? Will Abhi be able to forget the promise given to his mother and move on? With these thoughts making me even more restless, the sun rose early on Saturday.

I woke up at 6 a.m. without an alarm on Saturday. It was the love alarm that woke me up so early. I checked my phone. He had left Mumbai at 6 a.m. I went to the kitchen to help my mother to cook. We were expecting him to be there at breakfast. I got a call from his number at around 9 a.m. My mobile buzzed on the dining table. It was Abhijeet.

"Hello, whose number is this?" said a voice.

"I am Sameer, Abhijeet, isn't it you... who is this?"

"Mr Sameer, I am Inspector Patil. Abhijeet was found dead in an accident in a hit and run case. May I know who are you? This was the last number he had dialled."

"What...??" I ran to the living room to search for my father. My mother was getting ready in her room.

"Dad, Abhijeet, met with a car accident on the expressway." The mobile fell off from my hand, the call got disconnected, and I sank to the floor in tears. My mother came running and held me close. I was badly shattered. My father was upset too.

My phone rang, and the special ringtone that I had assigned to Abhijeet stopped my heart for a moment

My father took my phone lying on the floor and received the call. "Hello, this is Sameer's father. Yes, Sameer was his close friend. Yes, we had invited Abhijeet for brunch. Where did the accident occurr?"

"He stayed with his mother... no, he did not have many relatives. Yes, sure, please let me know if you need anything," continued my father.

The moment he disconnected the call, I rushed to get the car keys.

"Dad, where did the accident take place?"

"Talegaon toll," my dad replied.

"Let's go, dad. I can't leave my Abhijeet there all alone."

Seeing my emotional state, my dad rushed with his wallet in his lounge shorts, and we left.

He did not let me drive the car. I was shaken inside out. Millions of thoughts were flooding my mind. I felt that I was, in a way, responsible for his demise. Had we not invited him to Pune, he would have never met with an accident on the expressway. He would have been alive today.

Finally, we arrived at the accident site. My feet started trembling. I had no courage to see my love in this condition. The police were at work, and his body was being carried away. I felt like running and hugging him there, but my father pulled me back by my arm.

"Son, this isn't the place. Let's go and speak to the inspector," said my father.

I could not bear the sight of Abhijeet's body being carried away in this condition. I winced my eyes, and tears trickled down. I saw the inspector coming our way and rushed to speak with him.

"Hello sir, I am Sameer, a very close friend of Abhijeet. If you need any help, please contact me at any time. Have you informed his mother?"

"Thank you, Mr Sameer. Yes, we have informed her."

I looked at my father, and he understood why I had been looking at him.

"Yes, call her and let's help her if we can."

But before I could call her, I saw her getting down a cab with another lady.

I couldn't face her as Sameer, but I decided to face her as Girish. I had used this name to meet her as a colleague of Abhijeet to help.

"Namaste, aunty. I bowed down to touch her feet."

She was weeping continuously and hugged me tightly. I felt so good for a moment, but she would have hated me had I introduced myself as Sameer.

"I lost my only son, and tell me why I should live in this world?" she sobbed, wiping her nose with the end of her saree.

"I can understand. We were very good friends. I will always have an empty space in my life now. May his soul rest in peace," said I.

She had no idea that Abhijeet had become my life and my reason to live. But I could not confront her with the fact.

"Aunty, please call me if you need any help. Should I register the case in the police station if you don't mind?" I asked.

The anger for the hit and run driver was simmering inside me.

"No, son, let it be. My Abhi is no longer there, so what is the whole point in fighting. Winning the case is not going to get him back. Not all fights are worth fighting."

How I wish I could fight this case, but she was right. It was not worth it. Abhi was not going to come back had the driver been punished. So I gave up the thought.

After speaking to her, my father and I rushed to do the necessary formalities related to the funeral. I helped her in the best possible way keeping my emotions aside at that time. Time raced faster than the light. I attended the funeral after a sleepless night and the next day as Girish. I settled his mother with some helpful women in the neighbourhood, and we returned home.

The moment I stepped inside, the mask of strength I had put on, slipped off and I felt my energy draining out of me. My head started spinning as the images of the funeral started flashing in front of my eyes. I could not believe every trace of Abhijeet's existence was now erased. Now I remembered how I had got the death certificate and done the formalities related to post-mortem. Every time it reminded me that he was dead. My Abhijeet was dead. When I had seen his ash flowing away with the river, I wish I could take it back home and bring him to life again. But this was not possible. He was gone, gone forever. He was one with nature now. At a point, I felt why did God leave me alive on this Earth all alone? Living life without him was not at all better than death.

Life had got so difficult for me now. I felt guilty breathing in every time. The guilt of inviting him here and, in a way being a reason for his death, killed me every moment. Whenever my mobile buzzed, I opened it to see if Abhijeet had WhatsApped me. Then I realised, the 6 a.m. WhatsApp was his last message in my life. Every time I woke up from my sleep hearing Abhijeet's ring tone ring. I felt like a living dead. After the post-funeral bathing ritual, I had not bathed for two days. I was not eating well. Every half an hour, I kept on scrolling our chat from top to bottom.

I was not even in a condition to go to the office. So, after three days, I started working from home. It was the first time in my life I had not texted Preeti for ten long days. I wanted to, but it felt like my hands were frozen, and so was my heart. I felt like I had no words to speak out my emotions. I neither shed tears nor smiled. I had become a robot who completed tasks given to him. I ate without a word and did not even ask my mother what she cooked. I had stopped speaking to my parents too.

After fifteen days, my boss sent me a long mail of criticism on my work, and I was blankly staring at my laptop. I felt no stress and no worry. I was painless and yet so pained.

I heard my mother talking in a low voice. It was Preeti on call.

"Hi Preeti. How are you?" she asked.

There was a long pause.

"What do you mean he hasn't been in touch?" asked my mother, almost whispering. There was yet another pause.

"Wait a minute... hasn't he told you anything? I am shocked. Don't you know Abhi met with an accident? He passed away, Preeti. Sameer is in terrible condition. I can't handle him. He has lost his life and spark in him after Abhijeet's death. If you speak to him, you will understand that yourself," I could hear her better now.

"Sameer is devastated, his boss has sent him a long mail, and it's something serious. Yes. But why hasn't he told this to you?" she said.

"He isn't eating anything, and he hasn't spoken a word with me for a couple of days... No, uncle will be late," said my mother in a low voice.

"Ok, speak to him," she said.

My mother came near me, shut my laptop, and said, "Speak to Preeti."

"May his soul rest in peace. I understand how painful it must be. It must be very difficult for you to face it. Don't worry, I will always be there for you."

"Preeti, I am sorry I did not message you. I had no strength to tell you about the fact which I am not able to accept myself," I mumbled.

"It's okay, Sameer. I can imagine what you must be going through. You can talk to me whenever you feel like it. I will always be there for you whenever you need me."

"I am feeling much better after speaking with you," I confessed.

"Sameer, don't isolate yourself. Speak out your grief to feel better. Your condition will only worsen if you keep things to yourself," she said.

Her soothing words eased a bit of my sorrow.

After an hour, feeling hungry, I stepped into the kitchen. My mother was surprised to see me asking for dinner. She served me with a smile. The doorbell rang, and my father joined me for dinner.

"Sameer, I feel so better to see you with us at the dining table after having dinner in your room for so many days. I am glad that you joined us."

"Good that you asked him to join us. I can understand how he is feeling about things, but none can stop the destined. We have no say against the will of God. We have to accept the pain and learn to move on," my dad said.

"Sushant, it isn't me. It's the magic of Preeti's call. She called me, and I made him speak to her. Sameer had not even told her about Abhijeet's demise. She hardly spoke a few words, and look how she put some life in him."

"Preeti is an amazing girl, I must say that!" said my dad.

My parents smiled seeing me speak after one long week.

"Sameer, you have become numb. I am so worried about you. Cry if you feel like it. Please don't suppress it. It will only make things difficult," my dad said, and I listened to it with an expressionless face.

"Sushant, his boss wants to fire him. He has got a second warning," said my mother expressing her worry.

"Mom, please, nothing matters to me anymore. Let him fire me," I yelled. "Why do I need this life or even money if Abhijeet isn't alive?"

I was drowning in depression. I had no idea what was going around. I wished I were dead. As days passed, my father started feeling I needed help. Meanwhile, my father got a medical certificate from a psychiatrist, mailed it to my boss, and explained to him my situation. That had safeguarded my job for now.

I slept during those days and stayed awake at nights. I had no reason and motivation to live another day. The breakup was something I had taken in stride, perhaps because I felt one day or the other, we would end up together. Though I knew we were no longer lovers, the small spark of friendship had that potential to reignite the fire of love. Nevertheless, we were still there for each other when needed, and it was still good enough to live life. Though the breakup distanced us, the emotions were still very much alive in our hearts.

We were disconnected from each other, but our souls and hearts could hear each other's voice.

47

A bright morning

Yet another week passed, and the sun shone bright that morning.

I was in a deep day sleep around noon, and the door banged wide open.

It was Preeti, she entered my room. I thought it was another dream, and I closed my eyes.

Whoosh She pulled the blanket off my body.

"Wake up, my boy. I have come a long way to meet you," she said.

"Get up! Your mom has made the yummiest lunch ever," said Preeti passing on her enthusiasm to me.

I smiled in my dream as she shook me.

I opened my eyes and squinted them for a better vision. It was Preeti standing in front of me. I could not believe my eyes.

"Preeti? What are you doing here?" I yelled

"Is it another dream, or are your really here?" I asked her.

"Yes, I am here in flesh and blood. It's not a dream, Sameer. Come on, brush your teeth, freshen up and join us in the living room," she said with a radiant, contagious smile.

I walked to my washroom sluggishly. I washed my face after ages. I looked at my reflection in the mirror. My hair was messed up, and I had bags under my eyes. The dark circles around my eyes spoke of many tearful and sleepless nights. In spite of this, I still felt better. It had been a week I had not combed my hair. I felt better after seeing myself as a little presentable.

"Sameer, come soon. The parathas will get cold," I hear my mother's call. I walked to the kitchen with slow steps.

I took my usual seat at the dining table. My mother came out with steaming *Aloo Parathas* with *Mango Pickle* and *Green Chutney*. Preeti added some butter to my plate as my mother served me a hot steaming *paratha*.

My sullen face relaxed after smelling the aroma.

"How did you manage to come here? Your mother told me last month that you won't be here for another four months," my mother asked Preeti.

"Luckily, I got a job in Pune, and so, I could resign. It was no good staying there all alone. I was bored. My company was not ready to transfer me to Pune, and I missed everyone." she said.

"But what about the notice period? The policies are very strict, aren't they?" asked my father.

"Uncle, I gave a fake medical certificate. A gynaecologist friend of mine managed it!" Preeti said.

Even my sleepy eyes could not miss her nervousness while she spoke. I knew she was lying.

"Preeti, I am so happy to see him eat at this speed!" exclaimed my mother seeing me gobble up the Paratha in no time.

I looked at my mother and smiled.

"When did you get this new offer Preeti?" I asked curiously.

"Don't you remember I had given an interview two months back for a startup? I had found the job profile interesting," she said.

I remembered about that offer. It gave her no hike, had poor work culture, and a monotonous job profile. There was nothing good about the job. It was more like a demotion in her case. No person would have left an existing lucrative job for a low profile position like this. She was even overqualified for this offer. I was shocked when she said she found it interesting. Now I knew she had come back because I needed her. She had come here only for me.

"Don't worry, aunty, I will pay off Sameer's emotional debt and give you your son back," said Preeti, and the chain of my thoughts broke.

"Preeti, our hopes lie only in you. No one in this world knows how to handle him in his worst condition better than you," said my mom.

"Sameer, will you give me a chance to repay your help?" Preeti asked, pulling the lost me in their conversation.

"Preeti, why are you using these words? Obligation, pay off, repay...?"

"We have been friends and do hold that right over each other," I said.

"Alright, Mr Sameer, will you give me a smile now? I am back in Pune. Isn't that a super thing?"

I smiled genuinely after a long time. I could see the emotion overflowing her eyes.

As Preeti went into the kitchen to help my mother clear the plates, I got engrossed in my thoughts again.

Preeti's sudden arrival had made me feel like a human. I felt alive. But at the same time, I felt guilty that she had given up such a good career opportunity just to ensure that I get better.

She had come here sacrificing the dream job of hers selflessly. She found her happiness in mine. Wasn't it love, sacrifice, support, finding happiness in others' happiness? Yes, it was. How did it matter what relationship I shared with her?

For a moment, I realised I was thinking logically after days.

I smiled one more time.

"Hey, Sameer, where are you lost? Why are you staring at the chair?" she asked, waving her hand in front of me.

"Preeti, tell me the truth, haven't you resigned just for me and came here all the way leaving such a good company?" I tried to confront her.

"It's just that I felt..."

I stopped her from speaking further.

"Oh, that one which you had got a couple of months back, right? Don't lie, Preeti, you came here for me, right? You were highly overqualified for that poor offer," I spoke upfront.

"Yes," she softly said with her eyes avoiding mine and looking at the floor.

"Let's go for an evening walk today, but from tomorrow onwards, we go out for a jog in the morning at 7 a.m. sharp, okay?" she quickly switched the topic.

"Be ready. And yes, what are you going to wear tomorrow?"

"Umm? Sportswear, what do you mean what am I going to wear?" I asked in confusion.

"Wear a smile, don't forget it."

I smiled and said, "Yes, I will... promise."

From that day, she took charge of my life. She had a week left for her to join a new company. So, till then, we were going to enjoy this week together. We went for morning jogs. We then had breakfast at my place or hers alternately. Every afternoon we read books and watched movies. In the evening, we stepped out of the house. We walked, laughed, chit chatted, hung out at our favourite places. After a long time, I started breathing again.

Relaxing in her company, I slept well for two days.

The next morning, my mobile buzzed. With sleepy eyes, I received the call.

"Come out soon. I have a surprise for you," said Preeti.

My sleepy eyes saw Preeti panting and sweating with two cycles, one old and one brand new!

She knew I loved cycling. Long-time back during my college days, someone had stolen my cycle, and after that, I had never brought one. I was so happy to see this gift.

"Thank you, Preeti. This is exactly like my old one. I love you for this!" I shouted in excitement. I only hoped the neighbours had not heard it.

That day we had a cycle ride to Taljai hill in Pune. We came back home wet with sweat, tired, and hungry. My parents and her mother waited for us with a hot, smashing lunch.

The next day we both went to Mahabaleshwar, a famous hill station near Pune. In winters, Mahabaleshwar was heaven. It reminded me of some of my visits with Abhijeet there. Though I did not like feeding monkeys,

I fed some as Abhijeet always wanted it to be done. I felt his soul would be much happier to see me doing this for him.

Yet another day, we visited Lavasa, a beautiful place on the outskirts of the city. I felt so lucky that I had someone who took such great care of me just to bring me back to life. Five days with Preeti rolled away, giving me back myself. It was Preeti's magic wand. I felt as if she was really a fairy in the fairy tales sent by God to teach me how to live life again.

One morning, I sat in the living room, humming a song. My dad was having tea, and my mother was busy with some kitchen work.

My dad raised his eyes behind the newspaper that almost covered his face and said, "Good to see you humming songs after a long time."

"Yes, dad, I feel much better, planning to join back work this Monday. Dad, the leave you had applied for has 5 more days left, but Preeti has joined her office today, so what will I do sitting at home?" I said.

My father seemed to be engrossed. I was surprised why he wasn't happy to see me going back to the office.

"We are planning to join Zumba classes from the next week," I said, expecting a positive reaction.

He smiled but said nothing.

"I am going to join some LGBTQ organizations like Pune Pride and Indradhanu to get focussed on something meaningful," I said in excitement.

"I am very happy that you are on your own now. I never wanted my strong son to visit a psychiatrist," said my father, not commenting on anything that I had just said.

"May I ask you a thing, son?"

I had expected this kind of question, especially due to his no comments mode.

"Of course, dad!"

"Haven't you noticed that you cannot do well without Preeti?" he asked.

He continued without expecting my answer.

"Your plans depend on her office timings. Your whole life revolves around her. You have decided to re-join your office only because she is not there to spend time with you. Your life is so intermingled with her."

"Yes, dad, that's right. I am so proud of our friendship," I said with excitement.

"But, son, her love for you is conspicuous in her eyes? Her involvement in you is very obvious. I think it might complicate your friendship. It would be very unfair with her if she truly loves you," my dad expressed his sincere emotions.

"That's right dad, I had a doubt about that. But now, even I know she loves me. Preeti's love for me transcends all boundaries. Our friendship had been tested under different situations. You know, when I was rejected by Tanmay, I dated random men, and when I fell for Abhijeet, she had her mood swings. At times she taunted me, she was sarcastic, and she fought with me. Despite all these complications, we still share that eternal, unbreakable bond!" I said.

"Have you ever realised how much pain she must have gone through? She switched her job for you. She sacrificed her career for you."

"I know… poor soul, dad, but I can give her nothing but my friendship," said I.

"That is why I am worried about her. She unconditionally cares for you, and I naturally care for the person who cares for you. You need to decide on how you are going to take this ahead. Don't let this girl take more pains for you if you can't give back to her the love she deserves. Don't you think she should remarry rather than getting involved in you? Don't you think it is important for her to live a happy life?" asked my dad.

"Dad, I have tried to convince her to remarry several times. But she is stubborn, and she finds no suitable man."

"Son, don't forget why she feels so. The reason is she loves you, and she would have certainly married you had you not been gay."

"I know. Life is so complex. When you have love in your life, destiny takes it away. When someone loves you, you don't," I sighed.

"You love her as a friend while she loves you the way a straight girl loves a boy. Just imagine how difficult life is for her!"

"But if I distance her from me, she will feel bad," I added

"Son, so you will have to find and set that appropriate comfortable distance in between you both," he suggested.

"I will think about this and do what would be the best for us," said I.

It was my time to think about my life very seriously. I had to choose something and sacrifice something at the same time. I had seen in my life how people sacrificed things for their loved ones. Just the way Abhijeet had sacrificed me for his mother, I had given up our relationship to respect his decision. At the same time, Preeti had let her love for me grow unconditionally, accepting the dead end in her life. I saluted the girl's love in my mind and smiled.

I really wished I could make her happy. But how I wondered? Was there a way I could ensure my happiness as well as hers?

48

The biggest surprise

The conversation with my father left me pondering. Memories with Preeti flashed in front of my worried eyes. Her deep concerns for me, which once assuaged me at my worst, upset me now. We loved each other but in different ways. Our lives were so intermingled, making us inseparable. Had we continued interacting like this, maybe at a point, she would feel hurt, and our friendship would get affected. I had understood well, that neither I could break our friendship nor I could continue being this close to her. If I created a distance, it would hurt her, and if I let us get closer, it would hurt her too. In both situations, her hurt was going to give me intense pain. Dad was right, I had to find a way, but how? The whole night I kept thinking and did not know when I fell asleep, but before I slept, I had made it a point to switch on the alarm.

The next morning, I was woken up by the buzz of my ringing alarm. It was 7 a.m. I was in a hurry. I wore my track pants and t-shirt, took my keys, wallet and rushed to Preeti's house.

Preeti opened the door with sleepy eyes and messed up hair, yawning. I heard her mother making tea.

"Sameer? What are you doing here at this hour? Please come in," she said with dozy eyes.

"Preeti, I thought, why shouldn't I come and wake you up for a change. It's you who come to me every evening. Let's go out and breathe some fresh air. There were unseasonal rains last night. Let's go out!" I said, smiling.

Preeti was still sleepy. Aunty came out. "Come in, sit. Would you like to have some tea?" she asked.

"No, aunty, later. Today I am taking Preeti out for a walk. I want her to breathe some fresh air and feel better. You know, aunty, she has taken so much effort to bring me back to normal after Abhijeet's death. Even I want to make her smile, taking her out of the boring hectic schedule. I owe her that," I politely said.

"Good, here she comes," said her mother.

Preeti was wearing her sports shoes, tying a lace. She looked at me and smiled, saying, "Thanks for coming. I needed a push to lose weight. Let's go!"

We left jogging, her high ponytail wobbling in the rhythm of our jog. We traced our regular path once. Tired, I stopped to sit near the bench. She joined me.

"I want to give you good news," I said, panting heavily.

"But I would want you to come with me for that," I said.

"I will come with you. Tell me what is it!" she said in excitement.

"Alright, you wait here. I will get my bike, and we'll go there," I said.

"Cool," she shrugged! She was clueless about where I was going to take her.

She waited and kept looking at me till I disappeared towards my house.

Vroom I parked my bike near her.

"Sit," I said with a smile.

There we went. After ten minutes, she asked, "Sameer, where are we going, and how far is it?"

"It will take another half an hour to reach the place," said I.

"Place? Where is it and how far?" she asked, feeling totally baffled.

It must be more than 15 kilometres, why are we heading in the direction of my company?

I took a sharp left, and I parked my bike below a decent residential building. The society had a gated community, parking, garden, and gym. I rushed in towards the lift, and she followed me.

"Get into the lift." I gestured as the automated lift opened.

Floor 7

We stepped out.

"Why are we here?" she asked curiously.

A little wait and we arrived at flat no. 707.

"Surprise...surprise!" I said in a singy-songy tone.

"Oh, I can't believe this! Is this your house? When did you buy this house?" she asked.

"After Abhijeet proposed me," I said.

"I understand how you must be feeling about this place without him," she sadly said.

"Yes, I do miss him, but now I think God wanted me to stay here with my family," I said.

"It's good you have got over with your past and have become more optimistic about life. Good to see you this way, Sameer," she said.

I showed her the beautiful interiors of my cosy house. I took her around the 2 BHK flat.

We reached the terrace balcony. It had a beautiful view. A breeze blew the hair on her face, and she smiled.

"The house is so beautiful, Sameer."

"Thanks, Pri," I said.

"Wait, I will show you the kitchen and the other balcony," I said.

She seemed to be very happy, and suddenly her smile disappeared.

"Hey Preeti, what happened to you? You look sad," I said.

"After you shift to this place, I will miss our frequent meetings and morning walks," she said, feeling downhearted.

"Nevermind, I will come to meet you while coming back from my office," she said as her sad eyes avoided facing mine.

"By the way, I loved this terrace balcony. We will have coffee at this place," she said, changing the topic.

"We can also have it in the other one. Didn't like it?" I asked.

"Oh, ok, if it's yours, then I don't mind," said Preeti.

"Let's take a selfie here." I said.

After we took a selfie, she asked, "So when are you planning to shift here?"

"It depends on you, Preeti," I said.

"Oh yes, you will need my help. I can come one weekend. I can understand it would be difficult for aunty to do it all alone." she said.

"What do you think, which bedroom should I use?" I asked.

"Uncle and aunty would use the bigger one, right? So, you take the other one," she said.

"They won't be staying with me," I declared.

"What? Why??" she asked, wondering.

"Because it is my home!" said I.

"How mean of you, Sameer. How can you treat your parents this way? They are so supportive. You are blessed to get parents like them. What would you do here all alone? Have you gone mad?" said Preeti.

"Well, I think my plan would certainly make my father happy. He always wanted me to fly out of his nest. They can come and stay here any time if they want." said I.

"Alright, so at least I can visit uncle and aunty whenever I feel like it! But seriously, I did not like your decision to shift here alone!" she grumbled.

"Preeti, I am not staying here alone," said I.

"Oh, then are you going to stay here to start that hookup shit one more time?" Preeti exploded with anger.

"No, Preeti, nothing like that. I have a permanent partner!" I said.

"Sameer, you loved Abhijeet, right? How come you find someone so soon? I can't believe this, Sameer. How can you be so desperate for sex?" she asked.

I exploded into laughter, and confused Preeti kept on looking at my face on the verge of crying.

"No, Preeti, I am planning to stay with a girl."

"What?!!" she was totally frustrated by now.

"Wait, let me introduce you to her," I said.

"Oh, so you have agreed to marry a lesbian girl as your father said," she said in an irritated tone.

"I will just show you her photo with me," I said.

"Good then, let's see whom this daddy's boy has chosen as his wife in a marriage of convenience," she said, hiding her pain.

I unlocked my phone and held it in front of us.

"Look at this girl with whom I want to spend my life."

I showed her the selfie camera. She stared at our faces with a sweet surprise that shook her in and out. She had never expected this.

"This flat is for both of us!! You have loved me unconditionally though I am gay. I am gay, and I will always be gay, but I would love you and care for you more than anyone else in this world. If you can sacrifice your bodily pleasures just for my friendship and companionship, why shouldn't I? Why can't I promise to stay with you like a companion but with commitment? I have realised, Preeti, that I can survive without a man, but I cannot survive without you."

I held her hand in mine and said, "I am so sorry for saying a rude 'no' to your wish to stay with me. I should have understood your heart Preeti. I thought it is such a foolish plan of yours to join us gays. Had I known you said that out of an unconditional love for me which hid a huge sacrifice, I would have never flatly denied it. There is no one in this world closer to me than you. Abhijeet was my only true love, and no man can take his place. I will never settle with any other man. Now that I have realised that love goes much beyond sexuality, and that is why I can proudly say I love you. Though not the way a man does to a woman, but certainly the way a human does to another. I see my family in you, so my life will always be incomplete without you. This home is for just both of us."

Preeti was stunned. Her eyes brimmed with tears, and she gave me a bone-breaking hug. Tears trickled down her eyes, touching the smiling bow of her lips.

She was sobbing, sniffing, and laughing all at the same time in my arms. Her head rested on my shoulders, and I patted her head caressing her hair affectionately. She looked as fresh as the blooming flower of the spring, and her radiant smile on a blushing face said everything that I wanted to hear.

* * *

CPSIA information can be obtained
at www.ICGtesting.com
Printed in the USA
LVHW030135210323
742063LV00002B/629